Showdown at Salt Creek

STEVEN GRAY

ROBERT HALE · LONDON

First published in Great Britain 2004

ISBN 0 7090 7438 7

Robert Hale Limited
Clerkenwell House
Clerkenwell Green
London EC1R 0HT

Typeset by
Derek Doyle & Associates, Liverpool.
Printed and bound in Great Britain by
Antony Rowe Limited, Wiltshire

CHAPTER ONE

'Well, boys, this is it.'

Grant and Lonnie Cunningham looked at one another, dismay on their faces.

This was Salt Creek?

After enduring such a long and tedious journey, they had expected to find a decent town and a certain amount of comfort at the end of it. Not a long stretch of practically nothing in the middle of nowhere.

In one of his few badly written and worse-spelled letters, Uncle Jethro had hinted that the small community was prosperous and forward-looking. Seeing it, Grant wondered if the old man knew what he was talking about or whether he'd been drinking moonshine.

The wagon-driver chuckled. 'Don't think much of it, eh boys?' He hawked and spat out a stream of yellow tobacco juice. It landed neatly between the ears of the two mules pulling the wagon.

Again Grant and Lonnie looked at one another. And grimaced. They had ridden with the man for several days now since he'd offered them a lift from the stagecoach halt. While they were grateful to him, for otherwise they didn't know how they would have got here, that didn't mean they were happy with what they considered his disgusting habit of not only chewing tobacco but, even worse, spitting it out.

'Are you sure this is Salt Creek?' Grant asked doubtfully.

'Yep.'

Grant frowned. Back home this wouldn't even warrant being called a hamlet, let alone a town. All right, maybe Uncle Jethro hadn't actually mentioned a sheriff's department, a doctor, school or church but surely he'd implied their presence.

The reality consisted of just a few adobe buildings. On this side of the wide, dusty road was a livery stable with a corral, empty of horses, at the rear. Next to it was a tiny shack with the title REAL ESTATE over the door. Clearly it wasn't doing very well for its windows were boarded up.

Almost opposite was a long, low trader's store, with some work-buildings and another corral behind it. Along one wall ran a tiny vegetable garden, shaded by a wilting cottonwood tree.

Some way off stood a saloon whose false-front was garishly decorated with the words THE STEER'S HORNS. Next to it was a house with a porch running all the way round it. Beyond that came a couple of vacant lots, then two more very small houses.

Wooden sidewalks were erected in front of the buildings, whose roofs protruded out over them, offering welcome shade. Outside saloon and store were hitching rails.

That was it.

There wasn't even any sign of the creek after which the place was called, although about half a mile away across the flat scrub a line of cottonwoods perhaps marked its presence.

'All the comforts of home.' With another chuckle, the driver swung the wagon towards the store.

'Grant?' Lonnie said uncertainly.

Grant shrugged. It wasn't his fault that where they'd ended up was nothing like what they thought it would be. Although he had a feeling he was going to get the blame.

For the first time on the journey, the mules pricked up their ears. Without further direction they plodded down the side of the building and turned into the corral's open gate and came to a halt.

The two young men were glad to climb down from the hard, swaying seat and stretch their legs.

'Mules'll be OK for a while. Let's go inside. Folks'll be right interested in meeting the pair of you.' The driver grinned. He obviously wanted to be present at the time.

It was also a relief to get out of the hot sun, which seemed to burn constantly and fiercely out of the vast, blue Arizonian sky.

The store had just two low windows, so that inside it was both cool and dark. It was crowded with goods of all kinds and descriptions: from animal skins and furs to denim jeans and leather vests, jars of molasses, tinned food and tobacco, guns, saddles and farming equipment. Everything, in fact, that those living on the frontier could need or want.

For a few moments Grant and Lonnie stood blinking until their eyes became accustomed to the meagre light. Then they made out a man standing behind the counter at the far end of the store. A girl of about eighteen was by his side.

The wagon-driver said, 'This here is Robert Kent. He owns the store. And his daughter, Iris. Bob, I done brought you a couple of visitors.'

Grant didn't miss the amused glance that passed between the two men. On the journey West he'd quickly realized that he and his brother were objects of curiosity and fun: greenhorns. He didn't like it but he knew they'd have to put up with it until their novelty value wore off or until they'd proved themselves.

Neither he nor Lonnie bothered much with what Robert Kent was like. They were more interested in Iris, especially as she was a good-looking girl with brown hair flowing free to her shoulders, brown eyes and a full mouth. From their Eastern point of view they found it rather disappointing that she also had sunburnt skin and was wearing a man's check shirt and a very plain straight skirt.

Meanwhile Kent was staring at them, and grinning at their dark suits and matching derbies, white shirts with starched collars and laced-up shoes, all of which, despite a covering of trail dust, were obviously store-bought. The elder boy, he decided, was about twenty and the other a year or so younger. And with their dark hair, cut short, and blue eyes they looked enough alike to be brothers.

'I guess you two wanna be cowboys,' he said.

'Not exactly. I'm Grant Cunningham. This is my brother, Lonnie. I believe it was you who forwarded Uncle Jethro's last letter on to my mother, along with a note to say he'd been killed.'

Kent's expression changed from amusement to shock.

'What, back in New York?'

'Yes.'

'And you've come here all the way from there?'

'Yes.'

'Jesus! Well I'll be goddamned!'

Grant and Lonnie found themselves more than a little outraged at the man's casual swearing, especially in front of his daughter and especially as he didn't apologize to her. However, she didn't appear to mind, not even to notice. In fact she looked almost as surprised as her father, as if neither could believe anyone would travel the many miles from New York to Salt Creek. Having seen Salt Creek, Grant decided they were right to be shocked.

'We've come to take possession of the farm.'

Kent slapped his hands down on the counter.

'Well, well, I sure never expected to see any of Jethro's fancy relatives from back East arriving to stake their claim. I thought at most I'd get instructions to sell the place. Goddamn!' He looked at them again and, sounding doubtful, said, 'Were you farmers back in New York?'

'No.' Grant shook his head. 'Pa works as a clerk in a lawyer's office. And me and Lonnie were clerks too.

But when we learned Uncle Jethro was dead, the family decided we ought at least to have a look at the farm and the land.'

At least Grant and his mother had thought it a good idea. No one else had been so enthusiastic. At the time Grant had thought it would be easy. Eager to come West, he had confidently predicted that the journey, travelling by train and then the stagecoach, shouldn't prove too difficult. He hadn't taken into account the fact that travelling on the frontier with its uncertain timetables and the vast distances to be crossed, wasn't quite as simple or quick as travelling in the civilized East.

Never as anxious as his elder brother to leave home, Lonnie said, 'We might have made a mistake.'

'You might at that,' Kent agreed, causing Grant to bristle with indignation.

'Pa.' Iris touched her father's arm. 'I'm sure the boys could do with something to eat and drink. Then you can tell them about the farm.'

'Good idea.'

'We'd also like to know how come Uncle Jethro was shot dead and who did it.' Grant saw the look that passed between the other three. 'And whether you've caught the murderer.'

A table and several chairs stood under the far window. All of them, including the wagon-driver, sat down while Iris made coffee and cut huge pieces of meat pie.

As she poured out their drinks, her father said:

'Jethro usually came into town a couple of times a

month to sell some produce, buy a few things. Enjoy a gossip.' He and Iris shared a smile. 'When we realized we hadn't seen him for more'n five weeks, Iris and me went out to the farm to find out if anything was wrong.'

'So you found him?' Grant said, swallowing a piece of pie.

'Yeah. On the slope of the mountain.' Kent shook his head. 'Poor old guy. In his time he'd faced Indians, outlaws and harsh weather. Got through unscratched. Now on his own land he was shot to death. Don't seem fair somehow.'

'Who did it?' Grant demanded harshly.

'Don't know, son.'

'Didn't you try to find out?'

'Grant,' Iris said, reaching out a hand towards him. 'It could have been anyone. Rustlers—'

'We're plagued with the bastards.'

'Indians—'

'Unlikely. They're all on reservations.'

'Or a rival rancher.'

Kent glanced at his daughter. 'I don't think McGrath would do something like that.'

'But Vincent might.'

'There was no proof—'

'What about the law?' Grant interrupted. 'Didn't you tell the constable?'

Kent almost laughed. 'Ain't no constable here, son. Ain't got any kind of law here. The nearest law is fifty miles away.'

'Couldn't you send a telegraph?'

'Ain't got the telegraph.'

Grant sighed. Didn't they have anything in Salt Creek?

'I did send a message with a drummer who called in here. I dunno if it got through. Even if it did I doubt the sheriff will bother to come all the way out here. Ain't arrived yet, anyhow.'

Iris poured out more coffee.

'We found the letter to your ma in the house. Jethro often spoke about his family so Pa forwarded it on.'

'Didn't expect to see anyone, though.'

'Why?'

'From what Jethro always said it seemed he didn't have much time for any of his family and they felt the same about him. Except, that is, for his sister, your mother. He remembered her with fondness.'

'She was five years younger than him,' Grant said with a little smile. 'They spent their childhood reading stories about the frontier. She was the only one to support him when he decided to seek his fortune in the West. No one else approved.'

'He was only fifteen at the time,' Lonnie put in.

'Old enough,' the wagon-driver said.

'Uncle Jethro wrote to Ma a while ago telling her he was leaving everything to her when he died. That was when Ma and me decided the two of us,' Grant nodded at Lonnie, 'should come out here and see the farm for ourselves. It would've been nice to see Uncle Jethro too but before we could start out we got your note saying he'd been killed. Like I said, we decided to come anyway.'

Kent sighed. 'I ain't sure his idea of "everything"

will be the same as yours.' He didn't elaborate on what he meant. 'Still, I guess McGrath'll give you a fair price for the land.'

'Who's this Mr McGrath?' Lonnie asked.

'Who said anything about selling?' added Grant.

'I thought you're not farmers.'

'We'll manage. Before we left New York we bought a book.' Grant reached into his jacket pocket and drew out a thin book. Embossed on its red leather cover were the words:

HOBSON'S FIRST CLASS MANUAL OF FARMING TECHNIQUES

ESSENTIAL FOR SUCCESS ON THE WESTERN PLAINS.

'Hmm.' Kent picked it up and flicked through the pages. He grinned. 'Mebbe you'd better sell up, son.'

'No.' Grant snatched the book back and refused to look at Lonnie who'd warned him the information it contained might not be of much use.

'Who's McGrath?' Lonnie repeated.

'Morgan McGrath.'

Iris wrinkled her nose in disgust. 'And his son, Vincent.'

'McGrath owns the Circle M ranch. Biggest spread for miles, reaches almost down to the border with Mexico. He came out here soon after the end of the Civil War and through skill, luck and ruthlessness carved himself out an empire.'

'And he might have killed our uncle?'

'I doubt it.' Kent shook his head. 'While he's had to do whatever is necessary to hang on to what he's got, on the whole he's an honest man.'

'Which is more than you can say for Vincent.' Iris had little spots of red on her cheeks. 'He doesn't do anything except think the world owes him a living. And God help anyone who gets in his way.'

Even as she spoke the door opened and in a beam of hot white sunlight two men sauntered into the store.

'Oh-oh,' Kent muttered. 'Talk of the goddamned devil!'

CHAPTER TWO

They were clearly cowboys. One was in his early thirties, short but stocky with thinning brown hair and a brown moustache. His clothes appeared workworn as did his revolver and plain holster.

The other was about twenty-two. Flamboyant was the best way to describe him. He was good-looking, with dark eyes and dark curly hair hanging almost down to his shoulders. He wore tight black trousers with concho shells sewn down the outer sides of the legs and a black vest decorated with silver embroidery over a red shirt. On either hip he carried a gun nestled in tooled-leather holsters.

As her father stood up to go over to the newcomers, Iris whispered, 'Vincent McGrath and the ranch foreman, Brad Howden. Brad's OK.'

Followed by Howden, Vincent walked across the room, the jingling of his spurs loud and almost menacing in the sudden quiet. He slouched against the counter, leaning back on his elbows, and surveyed the room, allowing his gaze to linger on Grant and Lonnie.

'Who're the tenderfoots?'

Grant scowled, not so much at the words but the tone of voice. He knew Vincent meant them as an insult. He took it as one and took also an immediate dislike to the rancher's son.

Kent went behind the counter while Iris and the wagon-driver remained near the table. A stillness, an expectancy, was in the air. Lonnie glanced at Grant, dismayed to see the stubborn set to his jaw. He was dismayed even more when Grant got to his feet and approached Vincent, leaving Lonnie no choice but to follow him.

'They want jobs?' Vincent went on. 'What d'you think, Brad? Should we hire them? They don't look up to much to me. Probably wouldn't know one end of a cow from the other.'

Kent almost grinned as he said, 'It's OK, Vince. Grant and Lonnie here ain't looking for work. Meet the Cunningham brothers. They're here to farm Jethro Norris's place.'

The sneer was instantly wiped from Vincent's face. He straightened.

'What!'

'It's true.'

'But Father wants that farm.'

'When Jethro was found murdered, I warned Morgan he couldn't just take the place for himself. I told him Jethro had left it to his sister. These boys have come out from New York to claim it.'

'Then they can goddamn unclaim it and turn round and go back to New York!' Red-faced with anger, Vincent glared at Grant and Lonnie. 'Your kind isn't welcome out here.'

'Kind? What do you mean by that?' Grant asked, getting red-faced himself.

Vincent took no notice.

'My father isn't going to be any better pleased than me to hear about this. If you know what's good for you, you'll leave Salt Creek right this minute.'

Unfortunately Grant had never known what was and what wasn't good for him. He would have taken a step forward and spoken his mind had Lonnie not clutched his arm and stopped him. To Lonnie, Vincent McGrath had the look of someone who would react to the slightest provocation and given the chance Grant would be more than willing to provide it.

Vincent turned his back on them, as if the argument was over and done with.

At that, Grant pulled away from his brother's restraining hand. He wasn't about to have anyone ignore him.

'The land is ours. We've a right to it.'

Vincent swung back. 'Out here no one's got any rights unless my father says they have.'

'That so?'

'Yeah. Believe it.' Vincent shot a sulky look round the room. 'Isn't that right, Mr Kent? Back East you boys might have the protection of the law. Here my father's word is the law.'

'We'll see about that.'

Vincent's face darkened even more. Obviously he wasn't used to people arguing with him. He'd expected Grant to back down and he didn't like the fact the boy hadn't done so.

'Damn Yanks, thinking they can come out here, snatching what rightly belongs to us.'

Kent intervened. 'War's been over a long time, Vince. And neither you nor these boys fought in it.'

'Father did.'

'And aren't we forever reminded of it,' Iris muttered so only Lonnie and the wagon-driver heard her.

Vincent stared at Grant and, as if there was any doubt as to which side his father had been on, said; 'Father fought for the glorious South.'

Grant snorted. 'Which, if you remember, just happened to lose to the victorious North.'

'Grant, don't,' Lonnie warned. 'Don't cause trouble, please.'

Kent said hastily, 'Look, Vince, why not leave things be for a while? When these boys see the farm they might not want to stay there.'

Grant opened his mouth to protest but shut it when Lonnie kicked him hard on the ankle.

'I hope, Mr Kent, you're not taking the side of these greenhorns against me and my father.' Vincent's voice held a threat.

'I ain't taking anyone's side.'

'Best not. Best remember on whom your store relies for trade. Hey, Iris, sweetheart.' Showing off, Vincent took off his Stetson and slicked back his curly hair. 'You wouldn't like your pa supporting these boys against me, would you?'

Iris didn't reply.

'Especially seeing as how we're engaged to be married.'

Grant and Lonnie stared at one another, at Vincent and then at Iris. Surely not! If Iris's flash of dislike was anything to go by it must be obvious to everyone, except Vincent, that he was fooling himself if he really believed what he said.

Seeming also to believe he had succeeded in bullying everyone into silence, especially the Cunningham brothers, Vincent poked a finger in Grant's chest.

Oh lordy, Lonnie thought.

'As for you two tenderfoots, you make yourselves scarce and quick!'

On a rising tide of temper, Grant knocked Vincent's hand away.

'Why don't you listen to anyone but yourself? I said the farm belonged to us. And we're keeping it.'

For a moment Vincent couldn't seem to believe that Grant had dared defy him. Then he took a step backwards. Hands flexing by his sides, he snarled:

'Perhaps you'd like to back that up, kid.'

'Who the hell are you calling kid?'

Brad Howden spoke for the first time since coming into the store.

'Vince, they ain't armed.'

'Says who?' Vincent gave a nasty laugh. 'No one comes out here without wearing a gun. No real man that is, only a coward willing to hide behind the fact. A kid. So come on, *kid*, pull iron.'

Grant wasn't sure whether to laugh or not. Vincent couldn't be serious. Couldn't want Grant to go for a gun he didn't have. Couldn't be willing to shoot him over something like this, which was nothing. It was ridiculous. Then he saw the look on the other's face. He realized Vincent was in deadly earnest.

'Oh, God, this is awful,' Lonnie moaned. He glanced at Howden but the foreman made no move to stop his employer's son.

Quickly Grant pushed his brother out of the way. His temper died as quickly as it had flared with the knowledge that losing it could get him killed. But even though he swallowed nervously, was scared, no way was he about to eat humble pie.

Kent saved the day.

'Let's have none of this.' He came out from behind the counter. He was holding a rifle, not exactly pointing it at anyone but letting it be known he wouldn't hesitate to fire it. 'Like Brad says, these boys ain't carrying weapons. And they ain't used to our ways out here where arguments are settled with guns. And, Vince, I don't want shooting in here where Iris could be hurt.'

'C'mon, Vince,' Howden urged. 'These boys ain't worth it. Let's go.'

Vincent's eyes swivelled from side to side, clearly wondering whether Kent would dare to shoot him. His hands flexed once, twice, then the fire in his eyes died and he relaxed.

'Hell!' he said and swore nastily. 'You're lucky this time, *kid*, but you watch yourself. Next time there might not be anyone handy to wipe your nose for you.' He glanced at Kent. 'And you haven't heard the last of this, either.'

With this threat he marched out of the store. With a little shrug, Howden touched his hat to Iris and followed him.

Grant and Lonnie let out the breaths they hadn't realized they were holding.

'Jesus!' Kent placed the rifle back on its pegs under the counter. 'That boy sure is trouble. And, Mr Cunningham, so are you.'

'I didn't expect him to want to go for a gun,' Grant said with a scowl. Now that the crisis was over he didn't think he'd done anything wrong and didn't like it any better than Vincent that it hadn't come to a fight. 'What was it he said? Pull iron. What an idiot!' He laughed. 'Home in New York that sort of confrontation would have ended in a fist fight.' Which he would probably have won.

Kent fixed him with a steely glance.

'Well, son, just remember you ain't in New York now. You're on the frontier. Forgetting that could get you killed. Although I doubt if Brad would have let Vince actually draw his weapon.'

'And Vince certainly wouldn't have done so if he thought you had your own gun,' Iris added.

Lonnie's legs refused to support him any longer and he sat at the table beside the wagon-driver, who had watched proceedings with an interested eye, clearly going to spread the story wherever he went. Lonnie clenched his hands together under the table so that none of the others would see he was shaking. Grant was such a fool sometimes!

'We're sorry,' he said. 'And sorry that Miss Iris

could have gotten hurt.'

'It's all right,' Iris said with a little smile.

'You won't be in trouble with McGrath, will you, like Vincent said?'

'No, I doubt it,' Kent said. 'McGrath is fair enough.'

'Why is this McGrath so eager to get hold of the farm?'

'Because, Lonnie, there's good water on it,' Iris said as she began to collect up the dirty dishes.

'Is that worth making such a fuss over?'

'Yeah.'

'Why has Uncle Jethro's land got water and McGrath's hasn't?' Grant asked.

'Because it's close up to a mountain. The creek never completely dries up, not even in the hottest and driest of summers. Which it's been this year. And there's still no sign of rain.' Kent sighed, thinking what trouble that lack could cause. 'Water here is so scarce it's mighty important. Also, crossing the land would save McGrath several days on the cattle drive to the nearest railhead. You'd better learn these things if you intend to stay. I'm surprised Mr Hobson don't mention 'em in his first-class manual.'

'Perhaps Mr Hobson don't know everything,' Grant said. He sat down opposite Lonnie and grinned at him.

Lonnie hid a sigh. As usual, Grant had quickly recovered from his fright.

'Say, boys,' Kent said, 'is it true you ain't got any guns?'

'We can't shoot,' Lonnie admitted. 'So what would be the point?'

'Mebbe you should learn.'

'No,' Lonnie said before Grant could say yes.

Kent shrugged. 'You still determined to go on out to the farm?'

'Yes,' Grant said before Lonnie could say no.

'That case you'd better hire a horse and buckboard from Ray Brookmeyer at the livery. And you'll need to take some things out with you.'

'Farming equipment?' Lonnie asked doubtfully. He'd never had the same faith as Grant in Mr Hobson's book and he wasn't sure how two city boys were going to run a farm.

Kent shook his head. 'See what you think of the place first. No, what I meant was things like food, coffee, some flour. Clothes. And boots. Those fancy duds you're wearing won't last long once you start doing real work in 'em. You go on over to the stables and talk to Ray while I put together what you'll need.'

'We haven't got much money,' Grant said.

'Don't worry. You can have it on tick and pay me later.'

'Thanks. Mr Kent, how long will it take us to get out there?' Despite his eagerness, Grant wasn't anxious to start on another long journey.

'Couple of hours in a buckboard, I reckon. You won't have no trouble finding the place. Trail starts just beyond the butte by the creek and it's easy enough to follow. It ain't a difficult journey. And, Grant,' Kent called after him, 'you might think about selling. McGrath'll give you a good price.'

'No.' Grant's jaw was set obstinately.

'You might change your mind when you see the place.'

CHAPTER THREE

'Hell and damnation!' Vincent exploded with fury as he and Howden left the store. 'Hell!'

'Come away now,' Howden said. 'It's OK. Don't worry about them any more.'

Vincent took no notice. Hands bunched into fists, face bright red, he kicked at the post of the hitching rail so violently that his horse skittered nervously away. He grabbed hold of the reins pulling hard, making the horse squeal.

'Who the hell do those bastards think they are? Coming out here, from New York of all goddamned places, taking our land. Threatening me! Me!' He kicked the post again. 'And that damn Kent. Going up against me like that. How dare he? If it hadn't been for Iris I'd have taken the bastard.'

'Never mind about that.' Howden was afraid Vincent would go back into the store and shoot down an unarmed man. Vincent was often brave when the odds were stacked in his favour. 'Let's get a drink.' Which was what they'd come to Salt Creek for.

A stubborn look came over Vincent's face.

'No, let's go home.'

'Don't you want to . . . ?'

'No I said! I want to go back to the ranch. Father needs to know about this. Don't cross me, Brad.'

Behind the young man's back, Howden sighed. It was going to be a long ride back to the ranch with Vincent swearing and moaning all the way. He said no more. At times like this it was best just to agree.

'Just wait till I tell Father. He'll settle their hash.' Vincent leapt on his horse's back, dug spurs in its sides and took off at a gallop.

Morgan McGrath was a big man in every way. Well over six feet tall, broad-shouldered, barrel-chested. His dark hair was still full and thick and without any grey, despite the fact he was approaching his sixty-second birthday. And he could put in as hard a working day as any of his men. Which he often did: riding over the range, grooming the horses, raking hay. Up at dawn, late to bed.

He was proud to have fought for the South in what he called The War Between the States. He had a scar on his chin and another over his left eyebrow to prove it. He still wore the grey uniform of a major in the Confederate States Army when he wasn't wearing his range clothes. And now he was proud to be a rancher. A very successful rancher.

He closed the ledger book in which he was going over the accounts and stood up to stare out of the study window at his land.

The ranch headquarters had been built as much for defence as for comfort; necessary in those days when Apache Indians roamed free and wild.

The buildings – long, low ranch house, bunkhouse, foreman's hut, barn, stables and corral – were surrounded by a high adobe wall. Every window was small and doors and shutters were made of thick wood. Water barrels were placed in strategic positions and cellars had been built under both house and bunkhouse. Even these days McGrath made sure the barrels were full of water and the cellars well-stocked with food.

In the early days the ranch had been attacked on more than one occasion but thanks to McGrath's planning each raid was successfully fought off.

Vincent was always arguing that now the Indian danger was over they should rebuild the house in a more modern style but McGrath didn't see the need. He considered it a working ranch more than a home.

On the whole McGrath was satisfied with his life. Who wouldn't be? He had more money than he knew how to spend and everyone in the area looked up to him as its most important citizen. But happy? No. Lonely? Yes.

On the way out here, all those many years ago, his wife had died giving birth to their second child, a girl, who had also died. McGrath blamed himself. He should never have made her travel in a wagon when she was pregnant, forcing her to give birth in the desert with no doctor nearby when things started to go wrong. What difference would it have made to stay in the South for a few more months rather than insisting they should start out as soon as possible after Lee's surrender?

He'd had to leave them both behind where he

would never find them again. He wasn't a man for grieving but he often wondered how different things would have been had his wife lived. Been a calming influence on him. Been there for him to come home to.

And how different it would have been, would be, if his only child, his son, Vincent, wasn't . . . well . . . wasn't Vincent.

He loved the boy with all his heart but he surely didn't understand him. Couldn't figure out how Vincent was willing to indulge in all the benefits money brought him without doing any work in return. Morgan had always had to work hard for whatever he wanted. Had to risk his life sometimes. Vincent seemed to spend most of his time in Salt Creek, or rather in its saloon, and showed little interest in the ranch.

Was it because he'd been absent fighting in the War in Vincent's earliest years and had then spoilt him to make up for the loss of his mother? Maybe. Or maybe it was just Vincent's nature.

Brad Howden had worked at the ranch from the beginning and was now meant to be its foreman. Both men knew, without acknowledging it, that Howden's main duty was to watch over Vincent. Stop him causing trouble so bad that all of McGrath's money and influence couldn't help him escape the consequences of what he'd done.

Just as McGrath was going back to his desk, pounding hoofbeats caused him to stop and look out again. Vincent and Howden were returning from town. So soon? Something must have happened. McGrath's heart sank and as he sat down and closed the ledger he was ashamed to see that his hands were trembling slightly. With a heavy heart he waited for his son.

'What the hell do you mean, you aren't going to do anything about those bastards?' In a renewed fit of temper Vincent jumped up from the chair and strode to the window and back, hardly able to believe his ears.

At first he'd been pleased by his father's reaction to the news from Salt Creek. McGrath had sat listening, hands balled into fists on the desktop and had gone as red as his son, angry, not only at the unexpected arrival of the Cunningham brothers but at the way they'd treated Vincent. Vincent, a fluent liar, had made himself out to be the victim of an unprovoked attack. McGrath would never ask anyone whether it was the truth.

Not so pleasing was his father's decision not to do anything. Vincent had seen himself riding at the head of a bunch of cowboys, confronting Grant and Lonnie, guns blazing and his two enemies lying dead.

'That's what I said.'

'But, Father, why the hell not? They're going to take over what, after Jethro was found shot dead, you said would be our land.'

'Well, I was wrong. I didn't think any of Jethro's relatives would show up. But they have and the farm belongs to them.'

For the time being at least.

'But they're farmers!' Which in Vincent's view made them on a par with sheepherders and

Mexicans: beneath consideration. 'And you know we need their water.'

McGrath sighed. He knew that only too well.

'Brad's already talking about driving the cattle on to the highest meadows. Whereas the creek running through Jethro's land still holds water aplenty. Not only that but come fall if we cross the creek out by the farm we'll save ourselves three or four days' drive time.'

'There's no need to tell me things I already know. And for goodness sake, Vince, sit down. Your pacing up and down is wearing me out.'

Vincent flung himself down in the chair, slouching back, a sulky look on his face. 'You can't let a couple of Northern boys take what we want.'

'I don't intend to.'

'What are you going to do then?'

'Make them a fair offer to buy the farm. I'm sure they'll sell.'

Vincent snorted derisively. He couldn't see the point of buying what they could take. And he doubted whether Grant Cunningham would be willing to sell, at least not for what McGrath would consider fair.

'And if they refuse?'

McGrath ran a hand through his hair. He was no happier than his son at the turn of events. He'd put up with Jethro Norris because he believed the man would soon either give up the farm, on which he did hardly any work, or die of the negligent way he lived. Then he could move in. When Jethro was murdered, and although he didn't like the thought of that, no doubt it was convenient; he'd been ready to give Howden the order to move some of the cattle on to the land out by the creek.

Instead of doing so right away, thinking there was no urgency, he'd delayed and now perhaps it was too late. Because what could he do if these boys decided to stay and were determined to make a go of the place?

Go in shooting like Vincent wanted?

'It's not possible,' he warned. 'Vince, the frontier is changing. Unfortunately. To openly gun the boys down for being on their own property would, these days and despite our importance, bring the law down on us.'

Vincent didn't look convinced. And that was the problem. McGrath's objections had little to do with fairness or the law, he was scared for Vincent. Supposing the two brothers didn't back down at the first show of force? Supposing they were willing to defend themselves and their land? Supposing Vincent was at the head of the men sent to deal with the situation? He could be shot. Killed.

McGrath shook his head. 'I'm sorry, Vince, but I'm not going to do anything until I've had the chance to see the Cunninghams for myself and talk to them. I'm sure they'll listen to reason and be unlikely to refuse me. After all, what do boys from New York know about farming in Arizona? And I'll offer 'em top dollar. I can afford it, after all.'

Vincent opened his mouth to protest.

'No.' McGrath held up a hand. 'That's my decision. There's to be no trouble. Especially no gunplay. Do you understand?'

'Yes, Father,' Vincent mumbled but his eyes held a crafty glint.

He was determined that sooner or later gunplay would come into it. He would find an opportunity to shoot Grant Cunningham, that bastard who had the gall to stand up to him. In front of other people, too. Made him look a fool. No one did that and got away with it.

His father might be acting reasonably right now. With Vincent's sly help that could change in the not too distant future.

CHAPTER FOUR

As Robert Kent had promised, the trail to the farm was easy to find and to follow.

It wound away from the creek, which here was narrow and easy to cross, heading for the nearby foothills. Much to the relief of Grant and Lonnie, once they started to climb amongst the hills it became cooler, a slight breeze fluttering the leaves of the juniper trees. The trail continued to snake upwards until it opened out on to a wide valley floor with hills rising all the way round, the first jagged slopes of a mountain visible beyond them. The valley was covered with browning grass, a scattering of flowers and several stands of cottonwood trees. At its far end was another stretch of Salt Creek.

'Not long now,' Grant said. He turned the horse's head so it followed the edge of the water.

'It's very lonely, isn't it?' Lonnie was used to the streets and people of New York. 'We haven't seen one person since leaving town.'

The riverbanks were dry sand, although deep water remained in the middle of the riverbed; there was more water here near the mountain than further down. Juniper, piñon pine and cottonwood trees grew along both banks, together with thick bushes, flowers and clumps of tall spiky reeds. Here and there was a scattering of boulders.

Looming over it all was the saw-toothed mountain which they had seen earlier. Its slopes were covered with stands of ponderosa pine which gradually thinned out, giving way to scrubby growth and rocks.

After a while they saw a sandy reach on the other side of the creek, with beyond that more trees. Grant stopped the buckboard. It was a lovely spot. Quiet. Peaceful. Birds singing in the trees. Cool, clean water racing over white pebbles.

Perfect – except for the farmhouse.

'Oh God!' Lonnie exclaimed. 'That can't be it.'

Even Grant's heart sank a little.

It stood a little way from the river. Unlike Salt Creek's adobe buildings, it was made of wood. Or rather, uneven planks with gaps between them. Sagging steps led to a sagging porch. The door didn't look very secure. The two windows didn't have glass in them and the shutters didn't fit properly. By one side was a small corral, most of the poles broken, and an unfinished hut. On the other side was a weed-choked strip of land that might once have been intended as a vegetable patch.

Uncle Jethro had described the farm as thriving. It was about as thriving as Salt Creek. Even taking into account the fact that it had been empty since his murder it was doubtful he'd done much on it while he was alive. Not that Grant was about to admit any of that to Lonnie.

Instead he said, 'Perhaps it's not as bad as it looks.'

'Oh, Grant, of course it is! Look at it. It's worse. No wonder Mr Kent thought that once we saw it we'd be willing to sell to McGrath. There's nothing growing here. Nothing even planted.'

'We're not selling it to anyone until we're absolutely certain there's no way it can be made to pay.'

Lonnie thought nothing whatsoever could be done that would enable the farm to make money, but once Grant got that look on his face it was useless arguing with him.

'After all, it looks like it's good growing land.'

As if Grant would know good growing land if he saw it.

'Let's go see.' Grant clicked the horse forward and slowly they crossed the creek. He stopped the buckboard by the steps and clambered down. Reluctantly his brother followed him.

Up close it was possible to see that some of the planks on the porch were missing. And the steps creaked ominously as they climbed them.

Somewhat apprehensively Grant pushed the door open. They were greeted by a cloud of dust and the scurrying sound of small animals. A shaft of afternoon sun streaked in ahead of them and lit up the shack's interior. It consisted of two small rooms: the main living-room with a kitchen in one corner and a tiny bedroom.

'Uncle Jethro obviously hadn't heard of the saying cleanliness is next to godliness,' Lonnie muttered, his eyes watering from the dust.

Nor had he bothered much about furniture. There was a table made of split boards with packing-cases to sit on, two old armchairs with the stuffing coming out of them and the bed had a husk mattress and one filthy blanket. Pegs were nailed into one wall from which to hang clothes. In the kitchen they found a stove and Dutch oven, a heavy black iron kettle, iron skillet, two chipped plates, two tin mugs and three homemade knives. None of them very clean. Next to the door a shotgun rested on more pegs.

That was all, except for an accumulation of dust, dirt and rubbish.

Lonnie glanced at Grant, grimacing at the set look on his brother's face.

'We can't stay here,' he ventured.

'Well, hell, where else is there for us to go? Don't be so fussy. If it was good enough for Uncle Jethro, it's good enough for us. Once we clean up, anyhow.'

'Thank God none of the rest of the family came out with us.'

'Ma wouldn't have minded.'

Lonnie sighed. That was because she was as full of romantic ideas about the Wild West as Grant.

'What shall we do first? Get rid of the dust?'

'Yeah, good idea.' Grant looked round. 'There must be a broom somewhere and a pail to fetch water from the creek. If we don't finish by tonight—' another glance round, doubtful! '—we can always sleep in the buckboard.'

Luckily they didn't have to do any cooking because Iris Kent had provided them with a pile of sandwiches and a couple of bottles of lemonade.

'Don't worry, Lonnie, it won't be so bad. You'll see.'

'Maybe.'

Grant turned his back on his brother's doubts, went to the shack door and looked out, at the trees, at the creek.

'This is good land,' he said again, thinking it must be if the weeds were anything to go by! 'We can start clearing it tomorrow. Cut some wood. Make the house more comfortable.'

He was glad when Lonnie said nothing about the fact that neither one of them had much idea about manual labour.

'It just looks bad because you're tired. Things'll look better in the morning. We'll make a go of it.'

It was Grant who found Jethro's grave.

The Kents had buried him on the slope of the hill overlooking Salt Creek. The grave was a simple mound of earth, topped with rocks to keep out scavenging animals, a wooden cross at its head. Iris had told them her father thought Jethro would be happy there looking out at the land he loved. And Grant too felt sure he wouldn't have wanted to be buried in a formal graveyard when there had been nothing formal about his life.

On the cross, Kent had engraved the words: 'Jethro Norris' – funny to think that was his name when he'd always been known to them as Uncle Jethro – 'born 1824, died 1879'.

Murdered, Grant thought angrily, shot down. And

his killer still walked free. Would perhaps never be found or brought to justice.

Making sure that Lonnie, who was working hard sweeping floors, couldn't see him, Grant sat on the grass by the grave and remembered his Uncle Jethro.

Not that he could really remember him of course. Jethro had run away from home when he was fifteen, long before Grant was born. Long before Constance, his sister, their mother, was old enough to marry. But Grant felt he knew him because their mother so often spoke about him.

After Jethro left, his parents disowned him. Wouldn't allow his name even to be spoken; had destroyed every piece of evidence he'd ever existed. While everyone else agreed with them, Constance Norris believed her brother had done what was best for him. She envied him his freedom to choose his own path.

A few years later she received an almost illegible letter from Jethro. Somehow she had not only managed to hide it from the family but she had written back to him. After that they'd kept in touch, if infrequently. She kept all his letters and she and Grant read them again and again.

Jethro wrote of fighting Sioux and Cheyenne in Wyoming. He'd guided emigrant wagon trains out to California and Oregon and served as a scout for the army, both before and after the Civil War. Finally, he'd made his way to Arizona where he'd settled down on Salt Creek and become a farmer.

Of sorts, Grant thought looking round.

Three months ago his last letter arrived,

forwarded on by Robert Kent with a note that Jethro had been shot dead.

Much to the despair of the rest of the family, Constance, with Grant's enthusiastic encouragement and Lonnie's lesser eagerness, had decided she didn't want to sell the farm Jethro had bequeathed her. And soon after, the two brothers had set out to claim it.

Now Grant wondered if they'd made the right decision. He knew much of his information about the Wild West came from the dime novels he and his mother read avidly. Thrilling stories of fights between cowboys and Indians, desperate shoot-outs, gunfighters quick on the draw. The hero always won and at the same time rescued the beautiful young lady whose life was in peril at the hands of the villain.

Somehow the reality wasn't quite like what he'd read.

It was obvious Uncle Jethro had been prone to exaggeration. Salt Creek and the farm proved that. Quite likely some of the stories about his adventures were not lies exactly but colourfully embellished.

As for the farm, a great deal of hard work would be needed before any real farming could be done. Perhaps it would never pay.

And they'd already met one of the villains, who had been prepared to go against the unwritten code of the West by shooting an unarmed man.

But one thing Grant knew for sure was that he wasn't just giving up and returning home, without at least trying, and no one was going to make him.

'Hey, Grant!' Lonnie's voice roused him from his reverie. 'Where are you?'

'Up here.' Grant stood up and waved to his brother who was standing in the shack's doorway. 'What is it?'

'Get down here, quick. Riders are coming.'

CHAPTER FIVE

As Grant slipped and slid down the hill in answer to the urgency in Lonnie's voice, he wondered who was coming visiting. Then thought: who else could it be but their neighbours – the McGraths.

As soon as Grant joined his brother on the porch he saw six riders approaching the house from where the creek curved out of sight round the side of the hill. Their horses kicked up a low rise of powdery dust. They were cowboys, led by a tall, bulky man in Confederate grey. Behind him was Vincent McGrath and the foreman, Howden.

'Didn't take them long,' Grant muttered, wishing his heart wasn't beating quite so fast.

'Remember we're all alone out here,' Lonnie warned nervously.

'Yeah, OK, I won't do anything stupid.'

Despite his promise, Grant glanced behind him at the shotgun by the door. He wished he had time to grab hold of it. He didn't know how to fire it, didn't even know if it was loaded, but McGrath wouldn't know either.

But it was too late. The riders were here.

On another occasion, Grant might have been amused by McGrath's immaculate Confederate uniform: hat with a curly brim and eagle-feather, fancy gilt buttons, long sword hanging in its decorated sheath by his side, large revolver on his hip. All intended to impress.

But one look at the man's face as, raising his hand, he brought the others to a halt, made Grant realize there was nothing amusing about the rancher. He obviously took himself very seriously.

Behind him Vincent glared at Grant and Lonnie, glared at the farm and glared, it seemed, at everything, while Howden looked slightly uncomfortable as if he didn't really want to be here.

For a moment McGrath didn't speak. Instead, with an insulting deliberation, he looked the brothers up and down, looked beyond them at the shack, stared at the weed-strewn field and the broken-down corral. With a superior smile he allowed his glance to return to the brothers.

Grant went red, knowing that the rancher didn't think much of the place, nor probably of them either, and meant them to realize it. Lonnie put a hand on his arm and with an effort Grant didn't say a word.

'So you're Jethro Norris's nephews?' McGrath spoke in a pronounced Southern drawl.

'That's right,' Grant said. 'Grant and Lonnie Cunningham. And you are?' As if he didn't know.

'Morgan McGrath. I run the Circle M further down the valley.'

'Pleased to meet you. I'm afraid we can't invite you

in. As you can see the place needs tidying up. So you've had a wasted journey.'

'Father, you going to let him talk to you like that?' Vincent was half-off his horse.

'Wait!' McGrath ordered and Vincent slumped back in the saddle.

A couple of the cowboys exchanged grins. And Grant almost felt sorry for Vincent. Probably he was always trying to live up to his father's reputation and expectations and probably forever failing.

'Think you've already met my son?'

'Yeah, we had that pleasure in Salt Creek.'

Vincent scowled at Grant who obliged by scowling back.

'He tells me you've come all the way out to Arizona from New York.'

Grant nodded.

McGrath leant forward over his saddle-horn.

'So what do you think of it now you're here? I don't suppose it's what you hoped it would be. Needs a lot of work, don't it?'

'We're not afraid of hard work.'

'Doubt if it's the sort of work you've been used to back East.'

'We'll manage.'

'So you've decided to stay?'

'No,' said Lonnie.

'Yes,' said Grant.

McGrath smiled again. 'Bit of a difference of opinion there, boys. You know I'd offer you top dollar for it.'

'Thanks but no thanks.'

'This isn't good land to farm,' McGrath said with a little shake of his head. 'It's too dry in the summer for a good crop and too wet and cold in the winter because of being so close to the mountain.'

'But it is good ranch land?' Grant asked.

'Yes,' McGrath admitted. 'It would be perfect to add to my holding. Whereas you'll work hard for little reward. Just like Jethro.'

'Maybe we should think about the offer . . .' Lonnie began.

Grant overrode him. 'That's a chance we'll have to take.'

'Well, if you ever do want to sell—'

'No.' Grant stepped forward. 'Now, Mr McGrath, is there anything else?'

'Grant,' Lonnie muttered in warning.

There seemed no point in antagonizing the man when he had five well-armed cowboys with him and when Vincent looked as if he would be only too willing to draw his gun and start shooting them. Indeed, at Grant's words there was a stirring amongst the men as if they wondered what their boss would order them to do.

But maybe McGrath didn't mind Grant standing up to him. Perhaps it rarely happened. He didn't smile but neither did he look annoyed.

'There is one thing. How'd you boys like to come to dinner tomorrow night?'

'Father!'

Grant was extremely surprised at the invitation and his immediate reaction was to decline, as he didn't want to be beholden to McGrath in any way whatsoever. However, at Vincent's cry of objection, he abruptly changed his mind.

'Yeah, thanks, we'd like that, wouldn't we, Lonnie.'

Lonnie nodded.

'OK. We'll see you tomorrow. Seven o'clock. All right?'

As the men rode away, Grant said, 'Wonder what all that was about? I can't believe McGrath means to befriend us.'

'Me neither.'

'We'll have to go now. Find out what he wants.'

'I suppose so.' Lonnie sounded reluctant.

Grant changed the subject. 'How's the cleaning-up going?' With any luck his brother might have finished.

Lonnie frowned. 'I could do with some help.'

He went back into the house while Grant stood on the porch, watching until the men from the Circle M were out of sight.

On the way back to the ranch, Howden could tell Vincent was working himself up into a worse and worse mood. His face was reddened with fury, lips set in a straight line. But he didn't dare do or say anything until his father was out of earshot. When they arrived at the ranch, McGrath took himself up to the house while the rest of them rode to the corral to unsaddle the horses.

Immediately Vincent let rip.

'What the hell does Father think he's up to? Befriending those two bastards! He should be running them out, not inviting them here to dinner.

I don't understand him any more.'

Most of the others, young like him, influenced by him, wanting to be his friend, crowded round, nodding agreement, urging him on. They liked being with him both because he was generous in buying beer and because he was wilder than any of them. And who knew what Vincent would get up to? It might be exciting to find out.

Vincent threw his expensive saddle down in the dirt of the corral.

'Well, if Father won't do anything about those bastards, I will!'

'What?'

Vincent didn't answer, he hadn't thought that far ahead, as usual.

Howden picked up the saddle as no one else would and he didn't like to see equipment treated badly.

'Be careful, Vince,' he cautioned. 'Don't do anything rash.'

Vincent swung round so quickly he almost knocked one of the cowboys over. His eyes glittered with venom,

'What the hell is it to do with you? You're just the foreman here. You might give the men orders but I'm the boss's son and you don't give them to me.'

'All I meant was—'

'Oh shut up! I'll do what I want and nothing you say will stop me.'

'Please yourself.' Howden shrugged and turned away. Quite likely Vincent would think the foreman was scared of him but right then Howden didn't care.

He just didn't want any more to do with him.

Furious that the man should turn his back on him, Vincent spluttered, trying to think of a witty and cutting remark. That was beyond him. But he had to say something, couldn't let the foreman have the last word. So as Howden reached the stables he shouted:

'You're getting too damn old.'

It wasn't clever, nor particularly rude, and certainly not true but the others laughed at Vincent's words. Laughed, Howden thought with an angry sigh, at him. Christ! What the hell was he doing here? Letting an idiot puppy insult him? Letting Vincent get away with it whereas he knew he could easily beat the boy with fists or gun?

He should leave. Not even wait to give McGrath his notice. Just ride away. But as he rubbed down his horse he knew he wouldn't. He'd been nothing but a gangly boy when he started with McGrath. Grown up with him. Owed him a great deal. The rancher depended on him. It would be hard to let him down.

But he wondered how long he was going to be able to put up with Vincent. Or how long it would be before Vincent's temper made him do something they would all regret.

There was no way the farmhouse could be made habitable by the time it got dark.

Grant and Lonnie sat by the creek, enjoying the cool air of evening, watching the water running over the stony riverbed. They ate the sandwiches and finished the lemonade and then made up beds in the buckboard. It was still early but they were both tired out, ready for bed.

While Lonnie fell asleep almost immediately, Grant stayed awake for a while longer. He lay on his back, staring up at the black night sky. It was dotted with stars so large it seemed almost as if he could reach out and take hold of them. From somewhere close by came a coyote's howl, eerie and lonesome in the quiet.

Was he doing right, being so determined to stay out here despite all the obvious difficulties? Having to face the hostility of the McGraths? Yet it was such beautiful country. Had potential. And it was theirs. Surely it was worth fighting for.

CHAPTER SIX

Fancy *señoritas*, cheap tequila, crooked card-games. This was the life!

Pete Fletcher grinned in drunken happiness as he and his younger brother, Ricky, staggered, arms around one another, from one poky cantina to the next. The Mexican town just across the border might be so small that it didn't even have a name; might only be there to cater for outlaws and drifters like themselves, but it contained all they could possibly want to enjoy themselves. It was the place they, together with George Reece, the third member of the gang, always ran to when things became too hot in Arizona. Or when they'd sold the rustled cattle for more than they'd thought they would and had dollars burning holes in their pockets.

'Our money's almost gone now.' Fletcher thought it best to warn Ricky that they would soon have to leave and go back to Arizona and work.

'Hell! What about Josetta?' Ricky had found a sweet *señorita* he wanted to spend more time with. 'We had plenty a while ago.'

'We ain't had much luck with cards.'

As usual they'd lost much more than they'd won. And, of course, Ricky's *señorita* cost him a lot of money, wanted presents to keep her sweet.

'We'll have to leave real soon. Probably tomorrow.'

'OK,' Ricky agreed with a little pout. 'You're the boss. You told George yet?'

'No.'

'Wonder where he is.'

'He was goin' to get into another poker-game. Down at Pablo's.' Fletcher nodded towards the cantina at the far end of the short, dusty street. Pablo's was the town's ugliest spot with the ugliest customers. 'With luck he'll win enough we can stay another coupla nights.'

The two brothers grinned at one another. That was unlikely. None of them was very good at the game of poker, depending on their fellow-players being worse. And Reece had little idea of when to play or when to fold. The trouble was he thought he was a good player, it always being someone else's fault when he lost. And as he was quick-tempered and so fast, and willing, on the draw neither Fletcher nor Ricky cared to tell him otherwise.

'C'mon let's find him,' Fletcher said. 'Rescue him.'

'You do that while I go tell Josetta we're leaving. Kiss her goodbye. Give us both something to remember.'

'OK.' Fletcher grinned. 'We'll meet you at the brothel. There might just be money enough for George and me to enjoy a coupla the girls.' And if there wasn't there surely would be after their next rustling trip. He started down the street well pleased with life.

The three men, all in their twenties, had been together since their late teens.

Pete and Ricky had run away from an unhappy home where a bully of a stepfather treated them more like animals than boys. When their mother died there didn't seem any point in staying. They'd beaten up their stepfather, in return for all the beatings he'd given them over the years, stolen the few dollars he had hoarded and left. They weren't surprised when he sent the law after them.

Evading it they found themselves in a rough lawless town on the border where they met George Reece. He too was on the run after an unsuccessful attempt at robbing a store near to where he lived in New Mexico.

They were much the same age. None of them wanted to become a cowboy working for someone else, with the hard work that meant, nor a miner: mining was even harder work, or, God forbid, store-clerks. They didn't like responsibility. They liked girls and drink.

And what better, what easier way to make enough money to afford both, without being beholden to anyone else, was there than rustling!

At first it had been neither easy nor profitable. A couple of times they were almost caught, had to shoot their way out. And Fletcher was surprised to find himself, like Reece and Ricky, quite willing to kill to prevent being strung up. But then, unknown to the Fletchers, Reece had killed the store-clerk during the robbery.

Things changed when they discovered Salt Creek, and the Circle M Ranch. Vast. Hundreds of cows. Too large to be properly patrolled even by the number of cowboys McGrath employed. Even better, at times during the summer most of the cattle had to be moved on to high ground, well away from the ranch headquarters.

It was suddenly all too easy. Find out where the cattle were, ride to the spot, drive out twenty or thirty head. Sometimes the cattle weren't even missed. And as McGrath had so much – land, cattle, money – it hardly seemed wrong to keep on rustling from him.

Of course, sometimes the rancher sent men after them but in the hills and arroyos of the desert it wasn't difficult to avoid pursuit.

And the journey to Tucson, while several days' drive away, was uncomplicated: no rivers to cross, waterholes here and there, no other towns where the law might be alerted to watch for them. And near Tucson they'd already met a buyer. A rancher who supplied beef to the nearby Apache reservation and whose only concern was making money. He was always willing to buy cheap cattle so he could sell them for a considerable profit, asking no questions.

Ricky Fletcher made his confident way down to the brothel, which stood all alone at the other end of the street. It was the town's only brothel, although other girls worked for the cantinas and for themselves, and Ricky just knew that with his good looks and tall, lean body, he was its most welcome visitor. The girls always flocked around him. They might have other men as customers but they treated him as a lover. And this time there had been Josetta.

She was young, only seventeen, with black hair curling down almost to her waist, dark moody eyes, and a willing enthusiasm. Ricky was in love and he believed Josetta loved him in return. She would be only too happy to see him again even if she wasn't expecting him.

The tiny room where the girls waited for customers was empty. Where was she? Hearing the door open and close, the madam who ran the place came bustling in from the back where the bedrooms were. She was fat and ugly, although rumour had it that in her day she had been a highly paid whore, something Ricky could hardly believe. She looked flustered as she realized who had come in.

'Señor Ricky,' she said in her heavily accented English. 'We did not think to have your company again tonight.'

'We're leaving town. I came to say goodbye to Josetta. Where the hell is she?'

'She is—'

'Why ain't she here waiting for me?'

'*Señor*—'

Ricky pushed his way past the madam.

'*Señor*, no, wait!'

She tried to grab his arm but Ricky knocked her hand away and gave her a shove that sent her sprawling. Without stopping to see if she was all right, not caring, he strode down the corridor beyond. This was lined with doors leading to the bedrooms, which were little more than cubbyholes, big enough only for a bed and a chair.

He was suddenly worried and very angry. This was a brothel. Men came here to be with the girls. And Josetta was nowhere around. She'd better not be with a man! She was his. His alone. She had promised she would wait for him.

He thrust open the door to her room and came to a halt. Josetta was there. And with a man. A Mexican! They were both sprawled naked on top of the bed. No! No! No!

At his entrance, startled at the intrusion, both Josetta and the Mexican sat up. Josetta let out a petrified scream while the man demanded, 'What is this?'

It was the last thing he ever said.

Ricky shouted, 'You bastard! She's my girl!'

And in a smooth, fast movement he drew his Colt and fired three times. The bullets struck the Mexican in the chest. Blood spurted over Josetta and the bed as the man fell back on to the pillow, sightless eyes staring up at the ceiling.

Ricky pointed the gun at Josetta.

'No, Ricky, don't!' she screamed, tears rolling down her face. 'Please. I meant no harm.'

With an effort Ricky didn't shoot her, although he wanted to punish her for her faithlessness. But even in his high fury he knew he couldn't wait around when he'd killed an unarmed man. A Mexican in a Mexican town. So instead he yelled:

'I'll be back for you later. And next time you goddamn be waiting for me.'

'Oh hell! What now!' Fletcher exclaimed as he and Reece heard a gunshot, followed by screams and cries.

'I bet that's Ricky. C'mon, he might need help.' Reece wasn't particularly concerned whether Ricky was in trouble or not, he just didn't like to pass up on the chance of gunplay.

The two men ran the short distance to the brothel, reaching the door as Ricky burst out, gun still in his hand. Quickly Fletcher and Reece drew their own Colts, although at the moment there was no pursuit.

'She was with a man. A Mexican!' Ricky said breathlessly on seeing his brother, as if that explained it all. 'I had to shoot him, didn't I?'

'Oh hell.' Fletcher glanced round.

Already men were emerging from the cantinas. If the Mexican Ricky had shot was dead, Fletcher thought most of the town's inhabitants would be against them. Might string them up. Although they brought money here, spent it freely, he knew that didn't make them – three white outlaws – popular. And while Mexican law might not be much, even that might stir itself over an American shooting down one of its unarmed citizens over a whore.

'Let's go, hurry! We'll have to make a ride for it.'

Not stopping to holster their weapons, they raced down the street. No one tried to stop them but behind them they heard the brothel madam screaming bloody murder, and Josetta just screaming. After that there were a few shouts and a shot that went near. They stopped to shoot back before skidding round the corner. Here it was dark, the few buildings shut up for the night.

Nearby was the small livery stable. They banged inside, grabbed up saddles and bridles.

'Hell, I'm sorry, Pete, but he was with my Josetta. She said she was mine.'

'Yeah, course she did.'

'C'mon, let's go,' Reece urged.

They leapt on the horses, yelling and firing their guns, causing those who had dared come after them to scatter for shelter. Riding through the small red-light district, shooting to either side, they were quickly beyond the lights and the noise and beyond the town, galloping across the desert.

CHAPTER SEVEN

Grant and Lonnie were awake and up early the next morning, which probably saved their lives.

Almost as soon as it was light they walked down to the creek and gathered up some wood, with which they somehow succeeded in lighting the old stove in the corner of the kitchen. It smoked and smelt for a while but then started to burn the wood satisfactorily. More by luck than judgement they managed to boil a pan of water so they could make coffee.

'What do you want to eat, Lon?' Grant asked, surveying the tins of food Kent and Iris had packed for them.

'Something easy to cook,' Lonnie wisely decided.

'What about . . .'

Suddenly Lonnie stopped what he was doing, looked up and said, 'What's that noise?'

Grant heard it too then. A distant pounding that seemed to be coming closer and was beginning to shake the foundations of the house.

Puzzled, he said: 'I'll go and see.' He reached the door, opened it and came to a frightened halt. 'Jesus Christ!'

'What is it?'

Cattle!

Twenty or thirty head of cattle were stampeding straight for the farmhouse. Were almost on top of them. The cows Grant had always been familiar with, and then only from looking at them in distant fields, were gentle creatures. These were Texas longhorns and anything but gentle. To Grant they looked huge, with wild eyes, lethal horns, steam coming from their nostrils. All enveloped in a cloud of dust. Getting closer with every moment.

'Oh God, Grant,' Lonnie said, clutching at his brother's arm.

The animals reached the buckboard in which they'd slept the night before. Knocked it over. Flattened it. Kept on coming.

'Get inside, quick!' Grant gave Lonnie a shove.

He was about to follow when at the edge of the stampede he saw two horsemen driving the cattle. This wasn't an accident. It was deliberate. It might not be a deliberate attempt to kill them, perhaps it was done just to cause damage, but killed they could have been, flattened along with the buckboard. Killed they still could be.

Grant shivered with fright then lost his temper. Without thinking of what he was doing he raced inside the house, pushed a scared Lonnie out of the way and grabbed the shotgun off its pegs. It was much heavier than he'd thought it would be and he almost dropped it. A determined look came into his eyes as he hefted it up and made for the door.

'Grant?'

'Stay here.'

Grant stepped out on to the porch. The cattle were jostling about outside. Were being driven ever closer to the house. Might flatten that as well if they were allowed to reach it.

He raised the shotgun and hoping it was loaded pulled the triggers of both barrels.

Loaded it was and it exploded. The boom was deafening and the blaze from the muzzles hurt Grant's eyes. The recoil lifted him off his feet and slammed him down with a painful bump on the porch. A plank broke beneath him and he fell through it on to the ground below. For a moment or two he lay where he'd landed, disorientated and dizzy.

Through the buzzing noise in his ears he heard Lonnie shouting at him.

'Grant! Are you OK? Are you hurt?'

Then Lonnie was pulling the plank off him, hands reaching for him. 'Grant!'

'I'm OK.' Grant managed to sit up. He was covered with dirt and dust. 'Help me up.'

Once he was on his feet and on the porch again, he saw that the cattle had veered away from the house, had charged across the creek, the two cowboys having difficulty in handling them.

He grinned and picked up the shotgun that had landed by his feet.

'Well, that did the trick didn't it? Boy, it sure has a fine kick.'

'You'll get yourself killed one of these days,' Lonnie said crossly. He was still shaken, not only from the stampede but from Grant firing the gun; he hadn't expected such a loud bang! 'That is if someone doesn't kill us both first.' He stared after the departing cattle. 'Who was responsible? Vincent McGrath?'

Grant shook his head. 'I didn't recognize him as one of the two bastards driving the cattle but I bet he was behind it.'

'We've made a real enemy there.'

'I know.'

Carefully avoiding the hole the broken plank had made, Grant stepped down on to the ground. Lonnie followed him and they went to inspect the buckboard. It was in pieces.

'Damn,' Grant said. 'We can't possibly repair it. Whatever will Mr Brookmeyer say? We'll have to pay for it somehow.'

'The cattle didn't do much other damage.'

The ground was churned up, the rest of the corral poles broken like the others.

'That's only because there's so little to damage,' Grant said with another grin.

Now that the danger was over he was enjoying himself. After all he hadn't come to the Wild West for it to be safe and gentle!

'We'll have to try and repair the porch,' he decided. 'Maybe we can use some of the wood from the buckboard. And find more ammunition for the shotgun. There's probably some inside somewhere.'

Lonnie sighed.

'You've got to admit it helped us out. Without it we might not have a house either.' Grant slapped his brother on the shoulder. 'Come on. Let's get some breakfast then decide what to do.'

Lonnie gazed after the cattle who were now barely visible.

'You don't think they'll be back, do you?'

'I doubt it. They got more than they bargained for. Anyway we'll be ready for them again and for Vincent if he does try anything else.'

That was what Lonnie was afraid of.

Vincent McGrath waited and watched from his hide-out in the rocks. He didn't know whether to be pleased or sorry. The stampede sure must have given those two city boys a fright. They'd probably never seen anything like it before. At the same time it could have worked out better. It would have been even funnier if the house had been destroyed along with the buckboard. Funnier still because the boys were inside at the time.

Still, it didn't really matter. If the Cunninghams didn't take fright and leave, he had another trick up his sleeve. One that would prove to his father he was wrong in befriending them.

He stood up and went over to his horse. He'd ride down and meet the two cowboys who were with the cattle. Goodness knew where they'd ended up. They were probably half-way to Salt Creek by now! He hoped neither had been hurt but he wasn't overly worried. Cowboys were paid to take risks and paid to follow his orders.

Vincent knew his father worried about him. It annoyed him to be treated like a child. Especially as

McGrath didn't need to fret. Vincent had a surly temper, which he lost easily, but he was no fool. He made sure he didn't do anything dangerous when he had someone else to do it for him.

It was early morning when the Fletchers and Reece reached the border. Fletcher paused to twist in the saddle and look back. No one and nothing on their trail. Not yet anyway. Just to be on the safe side they had ridden all night. Once they crossed into Arizona they could stop and rest up, knowing they were safe.

As they rode down the steep bank towards the waters of the Rio Grande, Ricky said, 'I'm sorry.'

He'd had time to think and he thought he was probably wrong in what he'd done. Josetta was a whore. Had a living to make. He was stupid to believe her lies when she said he was the only man for her. Doubtless she said the same to all her customers. It wasn't the first time his love for the *señoritas* had got him into trouble. He couldn't seem to help himself, however foolish he always told himself he was afterwards.

Reece, who also considered the boy foolish, said, 'You can always go back for her later.'

'No.' Ricky shook his head. 'I ain't bothered. Whores like Josetta are ten a penny.'

Hearing Reece sigh angrily Fletcher said quickly, 'Don't worry. We were leaving anyway. It don't matter, does it, George?'

'Guess not.' Reece didn't want to provoke an argument with Pete over his little brother.

'Anyhow, ain't it about time we raided McGrath

again and made ourselves a nice profit?' Fletcher laughed and the other two joined in, their troubles quickly forgotten. 'Don't want him thinking we've forgotten about the Circle M ranch! What about it?'

'Why not?' Reece said. 'Get some money so we can all enjoy the *señoritas.*'

'We should be there in a coupla days.'

'Then look out, Mr McGrath!' Ricky shouted and kicked his horse into the Rio Grande.

CHAPTER EIGHT

Later that day Robert Kent and Iris arrived at the farmhouse to find out how the Cunningham brothers were coping.

'Fine,' Grant said, ignoring his aching muscles, his cuts and bruises and the pain from hammering his fingers rather than nails.

'We've brought you some food,' Iris said, smiling at Lonnie, who hurried to take the basket from her.

Kent was staring round. 'You seem to have had some trouble here.'

'A stampede,' Grant said.

'Oh!' Iris sounded shocked. 'You weren't hurt, were you?' she added anxiously, looking at Lonnie as she spoke.

'No,' he said, helping her down from the wagon.

Grant glanced at them and grinned, especially when they both blushed.

'Don't worry, Iris, I drove them away with the shotgun. Mr Kent, while these two unload the supplies would you mind showing me where you found Uncle Jethro's body.'

Kent also glanced at his daughter. He often regretted the fact that they lived in Salt Creek, where she had little chance of meeting a suitable young man. No doubt, Lonnie Cunningham was a nice boy and they seemed to like one another. It wouldn't hurt to leave them alone for a short while.

'Sure thing, son, it's this way.'

'We won't be long.'

'What?' Lonnie tore his gaze away from Iris. 'Oh, er, no, OK.'

As Grant and Kent started up the side of the hill, Kent said, 'You think McGrath was responsible for the stampede? Or was it an accident?'

'Not McGrath, no.' Grant shook his head. 'He rode out here yesterday with some men but he was real polite even when we refused his offer to buy the farm. He ended up inviting us out to the ranch for dinner.'

Kent looked surprised. 'Really? You goin'?'

'Yeah. Tonight.' Grant's face darkened. 'But, Mr Kent, the stampede wasn't an accident. Two cowboys were driving the cattle and while Vincent wasn't with them, I do think he was behind it.'

'Quite likely.'

'Unfortunately there's no evidence.'

'Typical Vince.' Kent paused, putting out a hand to stop Grant. 'Look, son, even if you had cast-iron proof I'd advise you to keep it to yourself and certainly not to make it known to McGrath.'

'Oh, why?'

'Well, for a start he won't appreciate hearing anything bad about his only son from a stranger. He'll take Vince's word over yours. For another, out here people fight their own battles.'

'OK.' Grant nodded.

'And another word of warning. McGrath might be acting polite and friendly right now, and I ain't saying he'd do anything underhand, but remember he ain't got where he is today by being anything other than ruthless. Promise me you won't do anything foolish.'

'I promise,' Grant said without telling Kent that some members of his family said foolish was his middle name.

'And watch out for Vince. Don't turn your back on him.'

Quickly Iris helped Lonnie put away the food. When they'd finished they walked side by side to the creek to sit down. It was a hot morning, with little breeze, and it was pleasant to sit amongst the cool and quiet of the cottonwood trees. For a moment they said nothing, both feeling suddenly shy in one another's company and both being quiet youngsters anyway, then Lonnie sighed heavily.

'What's the matter?'

'I don't know if I can ever get to like it out here. It's so empty. I'm used to buildings and people. Iris, don't you ever get lonely?'

Iris put her arms round her knees.

'No, not really, oh, sometimes, yes I suppose so. But look at the land, Lonnie, it's so beautiful.'

That was what Grant had said.

'Is it?' Lonnie spoke doubtfully.

'Oh yes. See it stretches as far as the eye can see.

Nothing but trees and sky. While in spring and early summer flowers of all kinds and colours cover the desert floor. It's hot now but in winter it can be bitterly cold. Then when the snow melts in the mountains this creek will rush through its banks so fast it'll be almost impossible to cross it this high up. You'll see animals, deer, perhaps even a mountain lion, coming down here to drink. It's a country of contrasts and it'll get in your blood.'

Lonnie wasn't sure it would get in his. He wasn't too happy about the sound of a mountain lion either!

'I wouldn't want to be anywhere else.'

'But it's so violent. We've already been threatened. Suffered a stampede.'

Iris reached out to touch his hand.

'Not everyone is like the McGraths. Certainly not everyone is like Vince. Most people are friendly. They try to help their neighbours.'

'That's true enough of you and your father.'

'The others you meet in Salt Creek will be the same. And didn't people help you on your way here?'

Lonnie nodded.

'Give it a chance and you might come to like it as much as your brother does. Your Uncle Jethro loved it. Of all the places he'd been he made this his home.'

'What was he like?'

'A real nice person.' Iris smiled as she remembered him. 'Full of stories about the old days. Tall tales I expect most of them were but they made us laugh or kept us enthralled. And he was always talking about Constance, your mother, said how much he loved her and missed her even after all these years. Wished sometimes to go home so he could see her again and meet her two sons.'

'Why didn't he?'

'He wasn't sure how the rest of the family would react to him and he didn't think he could stand such a long journey. Worse, he was afraid that if he got back to New York he wouldn't escape it again and he most certainly couldn't stand living there.'

'I wish he had, though, because I wish I'd known him and, Iris, there are times when Grant wishes he'd been him!'

Grant and Kent walked up through the hills to the first slopes of the mountain until Kent came to a halt at the edge of a small meadow. It was surrounded by rocks and dotted with thick stands of cottonwood trees and ponderosa pine. The mountain peak loomed above them. Grant was glad to stop because it had been a steep climb.

'It was here me and Iris found him.'

'Where?'

'Over by this rock. He was lying face down. He'd been shot twice. In the back.'

Grant clenched his hands by his sides at the thought of such a cowardly act. Whoever had killed Jethro hadn't dared take him on face to face.

'The killer had to be lying in ambush,' Kent went on. 'It seemed to me he was hiding either in the rocks over there,' he pointed to a group of boulders a short distance away, 'or mebbe amongst the trees.'

'You didn't find anything?'

'No.' Kent shrugged. 'But Jethro had been shot several days before we came up here. There were no tracks, no sign left to find.'

Grant stared round. 'What was he doing here? On foot. It's a long way from the house.'

'Oh, he liked walking. Said he was used to it from the early days. Liked to study plants and flowers. Or he could have been out hunting. He had his rifle with him and there's plenty of game in the mountains.'

'But he didn't manage to get off a shot in return?'

'Unfortunately no. He must have been taken completely by surprise. And, Grant, if it's any consolation I'm sure it must have been real quick and he didn't suffer.'

Grant nodded. It wasn't much of a consolation but it was all there was.

'I wonder how the bastard set up the ambush? I suppose he must have followed Jethro up here.'

'I think Jethro would have known if anyone was following him. He still had sharp ears and eyes. I reckon the killer saw him starting out with his rifle and guessed he would head up here for this valley.'

'How come?'

'Because, son, it's the best way to go further up into the mountains. If he hurried he could have got here before Jethro. It wouldn't have been difficult. Jethro would probably have been taking his time, looking at this or that as he went.'

'It was just ill luck, then, or was someone watching out for him?'

'I dunno. But either way if someone was determined to kill Jethro they would have found the opportunity sooner or later. Remember he was alone out here.'

'But you've no idea who could have killed him?'

'Nothing that would stand up in a court of law, if we had such a thing in Salt Creek.'

'But, Mr Kent, the only one with any real motive would be McGrath, or at least his hot-headed son.'

Kent frowned.

'Yeah,' he agreed with a little nod. 'So you and your brother be careful, understand?'

CHAPTER NINE

'Do you think we're going the right way?' Lonnie asked. Without a buckboard and only one horse for which they didn't even have a saddle and bridle he was perched awkwardly behind his brother on the horse's bare back, clinging on to Grant's waist. 'We left the creek behind ages ago.'

'We must be. There's no other way to go.' But Grant agreed they had been riding a long while and there was still no sign of the Circle M headquarters.

'If this is all McGrath land it sure makes you wonder why he wants our farm.'

'Yeah, but, Lon, look at it. What little grass there is is burned brown. He obviously hasn't got enough water. At least not in these lower meadows. And we haven't seen any cattle. They must be in the foothills already.'

A little while later the ranch buildings came into view, all surrounded by a high adobe wall.

'Hmm,' Grant said. 'Just wait until we have something like this.'

Lonnie didn't say anything to that particular piece of pie in the sky!

Watched by several cowboys lounging in front of

the bunkhouse, they rode past the work buildings to the house, which was separated from them by a wide expanse of bare dusty ground.

As they reached it the door opened and McGrath came out followed by a sulky-looking Vincent and Brad Howden.

'You found us OK,' he said. Then, looking past them at the horse, added in a surprised tone, 'You rode bareback all the way?'

'Something happened to our buckboard,' Grant said, refusing to look at Vincent.

McGrath waited for a moment, then, when it was obvious Grant wasn't going to explain went on: 'Well, leave your horse there, one of the men will see to it. Come on in.'

The house was long and low with a covered porch along the front, and small windows. From the outside it didn't look much like the home of a successful rancher but inside it was a different matter.

Beautiful Indian rugs lay on the floors and the walls were covered with paintings of Civil War battles. The furniture was large and comfortable and the windows actually had glass in them, although there were shutters as well. McGrath led the way into a dining-room where candles were lit against the gathering dusk, their light shining on good china, polished silverware and a sideboard loaded with dishes of food and cool lemonade.

'It's a real fine place you've got here,' Grant said as Howden poured them out lemonade.

'It wasn't always like this.' McGrath sat at the head of the table.

Grant saw Vincent grimace as if he had heard his father's story more than once and was tired of it.

If McGrath noticed his son's look he took no notice.

'I grew up on a fine plantation in Georgia. It had been in the family for years and I never thought I'd leave it. But then the War came.' He shook his head. 'And when Lee surrendered, which he need not have done, there being still more than one battle left in most of us and with a piece of luck we could have turned the tide . . .'

'Mr McGrath,' Howden said gently.

'Yeah, well, I returned home to find nothing was left. The house was burnt to the ground, the slaves had fled and the land was overgrown. I might have tried to restore it but that was clearly going to be impossible with the Northern carpetbaggers wanting to grab everything.'

'Like Northerners always do,' Vincent mumbled.

Remembering Kent's warning Grant refused to be provoked. 'So you left?' he said.

'Yes. I decided to fetch my wife and son, who had managed to escape to relatives in Atlanta and were living amongst the ruins, and take them West. My wife agreed with me that it was time to start anew. To start a ranch. On the way here I hired a couple of Texans, one of whom was Brad,' he smiled at the man who nodded back, 'and together we rounded up fifty or so Texas longhorns so that when I reached this spot and realized its potential I had the means to start up.'

'And your wife?' Grant asked.

McGrath looked down at his plate. 'She didn't survive the journey.'

'I'm sorry.'

Clearly the man didn't want to talk about his loss to two strangers and he said quickly:

'It was easy to make money out of selling beef to a meat-hungry frontier and Texas longhorns are strong animals who survive and breed no matter what nature throws at 'em. But,' McGrath leant forward, 'I wouldn't like you to think it's been easy. Has it, Brad?'

'Not always, Mr McGrath.'

'At first I had to cope with the fact we were miles from anywhere. Salt Creek didn't exist back in those days. Anything we wanted that we couldn't grow or make ourselves had to be obtained from Tucson. At inflated prices I might add. We had to fight off Apache attacks. Luckily the Indians soon saw how well we could defend the ranch and being too sensible to risk their lives in a fight they couldn't win, left us alone. Pity but we can't say the same about rustlers.'

'Rustlers!' Vincent spat out. He looked and sounded as if earlier he had been drinking something a lot stronger than lemonade. 'We're still bothered with the sonsofbitches, aren't we, Father?'

'Yes,' McGrath said angrily. 'Mind you, more than one rustler foolish enough to be caught on my range has ended up decorating the branches of a convenient tree.'

Grant glanced at Lonnie. 'Do you mean . . .?'

'Yes, Mr Cunningham, I do. I mean the silly bastard was hanged.'

'Mr Cunningham doesn't look too happy,' Vincent said with a nasty laugh. 'Perhaps like some Easterners who've never troubled to come out here he thinks rustlers are, what's the word, romantic?'

'I never said—'

McGrath interrupted. 'Believe me, Mr Cunningham, rustlers are not romantic, they're ruthless. I'm not talking about some poor homesteader who might take a cow or two to feed their families, although they're bad enough, I mean those who rustle for a living. They destroy honest people's livelihoods and shoot to kill. I've had more than one hand shot and wounded just for doing his job. So, yes, I string up any rustler I catch. There's no law out here except the law we make ourselves.' He banged a hand on the table. 'Maybe that sounds a bit harsh to city boys like you two but it's a fact of life. I don't condone it but if it wasn't done I'd have rustlers running roughshod all over me and my land.'

'So, boys, you'd better not rustle any of our cows however hungry you get.' Vincent gave another laugh.

'I'm sure Grant and his brother know they can always come here and ask for help.' McGrath spoke sharply as if he wasn't sure whether Vincent was joking or not.

Grant, who wasn't sure either and who didn't like the idea of being on the receiving end of charity, thought it time to change the subject.

'Mr McGrath, have you any idea of who ambushed and shot our Uncle Jethro?'

The man frowned. 'No. Norris was a well-known if

somewhat eccentric figure around here and it was quite a shock when we heard from Kent that he'd found the man's body. Brad did go up into the mountains for a look round but didn't find any sign as to who was responsible.'

'That's right,' Howden said. 'It's difficult to figure out who would want to hurt someone harmless like Jethro.'

McGrath agreed. 'The most likely explanation is that it was some of those rustlers we've been speaking of. Perhaps Jethro saw them where they shouldn't have been or saw something he wasn't meant to. If I thought it would have done any good I'd have insisted the sheriff come out here and take a look for himself, ask some questions, but your uncle's killers were probably long gone by the time his body was found. And I don't suppose the sheriff would have had any more luck than Brad. Less, as he doesn't know this area. I'm sorry, Grant, but these things happen out here.'

'They sure do,' Vincent said, with a strange glint in his eyes. 'So you two had better watch out, hadn't you? Being all alone like you are.'

'Oh, don't worry, Vince, I can take care of things now I know how to use a shotgun.' And Grant had the satisfaction of seeing the young man go red.

Before long the meal was over and Grant could see no reason to stay on. He used the excuse of the long ride home and wanting to reach the farm before it got full dark to refuse to wait for coffee. He felt the whole experience had been uncomfortable and strange and he was curious as to the reason for

McGrath's invitation. It was unlikely to have been to befriend them. McGrath was hardly likely to want to befriend two young boys owning a poor dirt farm, especially when he wanted it for himself.

Was it to see what they were like? Whether he should bide his time because they were the type to give up and go home? Or whether they were likely to stick it out no matter what.

Or was it in some way a warning?

'What's the matter?' Lonnie asked as they neared the creek.

'I don't know,' Grant said in a worried tone. 'You heard what McGrath said about rustlers. Supposing he uses rustling as an excuse to string us up?'

'How can he do that?' Lonnie dismissed his brother's fears. 'We're not rustlers.'

But when they got back to the farm it looked as if Grant might be right, for there in what remained of the corral were several head of cattle. All with the Circle M brand!

CHAPTER TEN

'Oh hell, Grant, now what are we going to do?'

Grant didn't know. 'I don't think there's anything we can do.'

'We must do something,' Lonnie objected, looking over his shoulder as if fearing to see a bunch of Circle M cowboys riding up on them, ropes to lynch them already held in their hands.

Grant shrugged. 'What? We don't know how to handle cattle. Look at them, Lonnie, they're Texas longhorns! They're enormous. And dangerous.' The animals were milling about, snorting and pawing at the ground. Grant certainly didn't want to go near them. 'Remember the stories of stampedes on the cattle drives?' Dime novels were full of them and always resulted in the death of a young cowboy. 'Remember them from this morning? Anything could start them off.'

'Can't you scare them away with the shotgun?'

'No, I don't think so. They're close to the house. Close to us! They could run anywhere.'

'We can't just leave them here in our corral. I

don't think Mr McGrath would really believe we've driven them here to steal and then are so stupid as to keep them in the open for all to see, but I guess you're right and he could use it as an excuse to lynch us or at least force us to leave.'

Grant was scared Lonnie was right. 'First thing tomorrow let's go into Salt Creek and seek Mr Kent's help. He'll know what to do. And in the meantime we'd best hope no one from the ranch comes out here.'

'I suppose so.' As Lonnie followed his brother into the shack he added, 'Do you think they were driven here on purpose?'

Grant frowned. 'They could have strayed here, perhaps after this morning's stampede, but it's not very likely, is it?'

'Don't worry,' Kent said the following morning when Grant and Lonnie reached the town. 'There are several people over at the saloon who'll help.'

'How do you know?' Grant asked.

Kent laughed. 'Oh, there always are people at the saloon willing to help in matters like this! You two stay here while I go with 'em and we'll move the cattle back into one of the meadows McGrath uses this time of the year. With luck he won't even know they've gone.'

'Thanks.'

'Iris, can you manage the store while I'm gone?'

'Course I can, Pa.'

'Mr Kent,' Grant said as the three of them accompanied the man to the door. 'Will Mr Brookmeyer let us hire another horse and saddles and bridles? He might not want to seeing as how we got his buckboard smashed up.'

'I expect he will. He knows what happened wasn't your fault. Ask him. See you all later.' Kent walked down the dusty street towards the saloon.

They were just about to go back into the cool of the store when three riders appeared, approaching from the direction of the flats leading to Mexico. As she saw who they were Iris made a little noise of disgust in her throat and quickly glanced towards her father, looking relieved when she saw he'd almost reached the saloon, would be inside before the riders got to the street.

'What's the matter?' Grant asked. 'Who are they?'

'The Fletcher brothers, Pete and Ricky, and their pal, George Reece.'

Lonnie glanced at the riders. 'Are they ranchers too?'

'Hardly,' Iris said with a little laugh and a shake of her head. 'It's rumoured they're rustlers. But they've never actually been caught.'

The three men slowed as they neared the town and rode their horses at a walk up the street. There didn't seem anything special about them but at the same time they did appear very sure of themselves and they bristled with weapons.

'I hope they don't stop,' Iris went on. 'They do sometimes.'

But on this occasion as soon as they reached the track that led to the creek they urged their horses into a gallop again.

'I don't like them. They've never caused trouble here in town—'

Which, Grant thought, was perhaps because there was nowhere to cause trouble in!

'—but they have caused trouble elsewhere. There was a story of someone being shot down in Tucson.'

She and Lonnie went back into the store and when Grant, who stayed to watch the three men disappear over the rise, followed, he found they were sorting out goods on some of the shelves. Feeling a bit left out of it because they only had eyes for one another, he decided to take himself off to the saloon.

A saloon! Where some of the most exciting things happened in the West! Disappointingly he found that the reality of the Steer's Horns was completely different from those saloons in places like Abilene and Dodge City, which he'd seen prints of in the books his mother borrowed from the library.

Beyond its false-front it was very small. Just one room with a couple of tables and chairs in the middle of the earthen floor and a bar that was no more than a plank of wood laid across empty beer barrels. No paintings of well-endowed nudes, no piano, no card-games or roulette-wheels. And now that Kent had ridden away with those mysterious people who were always willing to help, no customers either. The place was empty.

Well, no, that wasn't quite true. A bored-looking young man sporting a beard almost to his waist stood behind the bar and sitting on a chair in one corner was an equally bored young girl. A saloon girl! She glanced up as the batwing doors shut behind Grant and as he went to the bar stood up and came over to him.

He saw she was about seventeen and quite pretty with curly fair hair and blue eyes and, Grant gulped, she wore a dress cut so low it revealed the first swellings of her breasts. He found his heart was beating quite fast.

'Hi,' she said in a Texas drawl. 'You're Grant Cunningham, ain't you?'

'That's right. How do you know?'

'Iris told me all about you and your brother.'

Grant felt quite shocked that a decent young lady like Iris should speak to a whore and then was quite shocked at himself for thinking of this girl as a whore, although that was what she was. He hoped none of that showed on his face. He didn't like being rude to pretty young girls. Anyway perhaps it wasn't so surprising. Salt Creek was a small place and they were probably the only two young women in it. Despite their different backgrounds they were likely thrown together, might even be friends.

'My name's Polly. Buy me a drink? It's so hot this morning. Two beers, Nathon. Come and sit over here, tell me about yourself.'

Grant hoped he'd be able to think of something to say. He ridiculed Lonnie who became tongue-tied with most girls but now Grant found his own mind was a complete blank. He'd never, ever, been this close to a girl who wasn't decently brought up or whose parents weren't friends of the family. This girl, Polly, promised things they never had or could.

'I hoped you'd come in so I could meet you.' Polly

smiled at him, making him gulp again. 'What do you think of Salt Creek and the farm?'

'It's certainly different from New York,' Grant said in what he hoped was a normal voice. He drank half of his beer in the hope it would give him some courage.

A wistful look came over Polly's face.

'I'd like to visit New York but I don't suppose I ever will.'

'Where are you from?'

'Oh just a small place in Texas you wouldn't have heard of. My folks had a farm there.'

'Do they still?'

'No. A couple of years ago when I was away in town they and my two elder brothers were killed by Kiowas.' She broke off and tears came into her eyes.

'I'm sorry.' Grant reached over to squeeze her hand, which was soft and small. 'What did you do?'

'I couldn't run the farm by myself and I certainly didn't want to stay there after what had happened so I sold it, cheaply, because in the circumstances no one wanted to buy it, and with the little money I had I came out here to help Nathon.' She nodded towards the bartender. 'He's my cousin.'

'And do you, er, well, like it here?' Grant blushed and buried his face in his beer glass.

Polly laughed. 'Don't be silly! You don't have to be so careful. I know what I am and yeah I like it well enough. It's a damn sight better than the hard life my poor ma had, looking old and ill when she was young and should've been pretty.' She paused, obviously thinking of her mother and the fact she was dead, killed by Indians. With an effort she smiled and went on, 'But there again maybe I wouldn't have come here had I known Salt Creek was even smaller than my home town! Still the folks are good and kind and don't look down on a girl for earning her living the best way she can.'

'I'm sure they don't.'

'Speaking of which . . .' With a grin Polly leant across the table kissing Grant on the cheek, making him blush and feel foolish again.

'We could just stay here and talk,' he said feeling very embarrassed.

Polly laughed again. 'Buy us both another drink and we'll see.'

Even more embarrassed Grant admitted, 'I don't know what to do.'

'Don't worry, honey, I know enough for both of us!'

'There, that's that shelf tidied up,' Lonnie said, standing back and admiring his handiwork and thinking he felt much more at home working in a store than on a farm.

'Thanks, Lonnie . . .'

Iris got no further. The door opened and they looked round to see Vincent McGrath standing there, together with three young cowboys. And no sign of Brad Howden. They glanced at one another, fear in their eyes, hearts sinking.

'Well, well, now,' Vincent drawled. 'Isn't this nice? My girl and one of the damn Cunninghams cosying up to one another.'

'Vince, there's no need,' Iris began.

'There's every need!' Vincent stamped his foot. 'You're my girl, not his. You should both remember that.'

'Lonnie was only helping me.'

'Seems to me Lonnie needs teaching a lesson as much as his uppity brother.'

Lonnie took a frightened step backwards. Remembering how eager Vincent had been before to go for his gun, he wondered what the young man meant. Where the hell was Grant when he was needed?

'No!' Iris stepped towards the counter.

'Stop her,' Vincent ordered. 'Her old man's got a rifle back there.'

One of the cowboys hurried forward and grabbed hold of Iris round the waist, lifting her off her feet.

'Let me go!' She struggled ineffectually.

'Stop that!' Lonnie yelled. 'Leave her alone.'

'Giving your orders now are you, boy?' Vincent sneered nastily.

He nodded at the other two cowboys. Grinning they quickly caught hold of Lonnie's arms, pulling them behind his back, making him grimace with pain. With a laugh Vincent slammed a fist into Lonnie's stomach.

No one had ever hit Lonnie so hard before and all the air whooshed out of his body as he gasped with pain and shock. He would have fallen but for the cowboys holding him. He was dimly aware of Iris's scream. He was also aware of his own fear, knowing that whatever Vincent wanted to do no one could or would stop him.

Then Vincent punched him on the jaw, again in the stomach. Lonnie fell to the floor and suddenly Vincent's fists and feet seemed to be everywhere, all over Lonnie's body. He heard Iris cry out again and again before sinking into a blackness so deep he heard and felt no more.

CHAPTER ELEVEN

Very nervous, Grant said to Polly, 'Let's go then.'

It didn't sound much of a romantic proposal to him but Polly didn't seem to mind. With a little smile she stood up and reached out a hand to him. Then stopped.

'Iris,' she said. 'What's the matter?'

Grant swung round. Iris Kent, a good girl – coming into a saloon! Such a thing was unheard of. He felt a moment of horror. But then he thought what was she doing here? Looking so upset.

'Oh, Grant,' the girl said, tears in her eyes. 'It's Lonnie.'

'What's happened?' he asked, going to her side, Polly close behind him. His heart seemed to flip over. 'Is he all right?'

'He's been beaten up. By Vince.'

Polly and her cousin, Nathon, quickly glanced at one another. Vincent McGrath – the cause of most of Salt Creek's problems!

'Is he badly hurt?' Grant had gone pale.

'Yes. You'd better come.'

'Where's Vince now?' Polly asked.

'I'm not sure.'

Polly glanced at Nathon again. He nodded and she said, 'I'll come with you.' She didn't want to be in the saloon if Vincent came in full of himself after what he'd done. 'I don't believe Vince at times,' she added as the three of them hurried back to the store. 'I think he must be mad.'

Grant feared what he would find. Perhaps Lonnie would be so badly injured he would need the doctor Salt Creek didn't have. Oh God, why had they come out here? Why had he insisted on staying even after learning of the McGraths' hostility.

Lonnie still lay on the floor. Iris had placed a pillow under his head and a blanket over him. He was unconscious. Bruises already disfigured his face and his shirt was torn revealing more bruises on his chest and arms.

'Oh God! Lonnie!' Grant fell to his knees beside his brother.

Polly knelt by him and touched Lonnie's forehead. 'He's burning up. We'd better get him into bed and kept warm. Bathe the cuts.' It was about all they could do.

Iris nodded. 'He can sleep in my bed. It's through here.' She opened a door behind the counter which led to a short corridor off which were her and her father's bedrooms.

Grant picked up his brother, whose eyelids fluttered although he didn't wake, and carried him through to Iris's room, laying him on the bed.

'We should have gone home,' he moaned, as with deft hands Polly took off Lonnie's shirt. 'This is my fault. I'm the pig-headed one and it's Lonnie who's been hurt.'

'You're not to blame,' Iris told him. 'The blame lies with Vince. I really fear he's out of control.'

Polly nodded in agreement. 'Iris, can you boil some water, get rags we can use. Grant, you'd better wait outside. This is women's work.'

Reluctantly Grant went back into the store and looked out of the window. He could see no sign of Vincent McGrath, for which he was thankful for he didn't know what he would do the next time they met. He felt like he wanted to kill him. What was he going to do anyway? If he didn't do something Vincent would think he could get away with doing whatever he liked. He might not stop at a beating in the future.

He glanced back at the closed door. Supposing Lonnie was so hurt he . . . he didn't recover? The minutes seemed to pass like hours as he paced the floor between the heaped piles of goods, hands clenched at his sides. Lonnie had to get better. He just had to. He couldn't die.

The door opened. He swung round, heart thudding, as the two girls came in.

'It's OK, Grant,' Polly said quickly, going up to him and putting a hand on his arm. 'Lonnie is hurt, badly, there's no denying that, but no bones seem to be broken and I'm sure he'll be up and about before you know it.'

Grant let out the breath he was holding in a sigh of relief.

'Can I see him?'

'Best not, he's asleep. Honestly, he'll be all right.'

Grant turned to Iris. 'What happened?'

Quickly she told him.

'Believe me, Grant, I have never ever given Vince the slightest encouragement or impression that I was his girl.' She shrugged. 'I'm not sure where he got the idea from anyway because even when he comes to town he rarely speaks to me and I've never been out to the ranch. I don't believe he even likes me very much.'

Polly said, 'He's so spoilt by his pa that he doesn't know the meaning of the word no. Probably, Iris, if you were in love with him he wouldn't want you. He just likes being difficult.'

Grant had come to a decision and now he said: 'I want to learn to shoot.'

Neither girl tried to dissuade him. They were both frontier-born and bred and knew guns were a part of their way of life. Iris went over to a locked glass cabinet behind the counter. It held revolvers and ammunition. She unlocked it and picked out a Colt .45.

'It's called a Peacemaker,' she said, giving it to Grant. 'It's about the easiest gun to learn to use and to handle.'

Polly nodded. 'Do you know anything about guns?'

Grant shook his head. He'd read a lot about them but that was hardly what Polly meant.

'I've only ever fired Uncle Jethro's shotgun.' He didn't tell them how doing so had knocked him off his feet.

'I'll teach you while Iris looks after Lonnie.'

Polly looked at Iris, who nodded and said:

'You can go into the yard. It's empty.' She gave Polly some ammunition. 'You'll find some old tin cans in the corner you can use for target practice.'

'OK, thanks.' Polly led the way outside. Once there she showed Grant how to load the Colt. 'It's simple. This gate at the side opens out and each bullet is loaded into a chamber. It takes six cartridges but it's best to load only five and keep the hammer on an empty chamber.'

'Why?'

'To prevent you shooting yourself in the foot!'

'Oh, yeah, I see.'

'It's also a single-action weapon, which means the hammer has to be pulled back and cocked before each shot.'

'Doesn't that take too long?'

'Speed isn't essential.'

'It's not?' It was in the dime novels!

'No. To succeed doesn't mean a fast draw, followed by pointing and shooting. You'll probably miss. The secret is to draw quickly but carefully, aim even more carefully and pull the trigger slowly. And Grant,' she added by way of warning, 'don't wear and especially don't draw a gun unless you mean to use it if you have to. And don't forget the other guy'll be trying to shoot you too.' Polly paused to see if Grant was going to change his mind about learning to fire a gun. When he didn't, she handed him a belt and holster.

He buckled it round his waist. The gun felt heavy hanging at his side.

'I'll line up some tin cans on the wall over there

and you can try to shoot them. Remember to take your time. Stand here.'

'Don't I have to be some way away from the target?'

'Only if you're involved in a shooting competition. These guns aren't always reliable so if you want to shoot someone it's best to get as close as possible.'

'OK.'

'Now draw the gun – slowly! – aim and fire.'

Grant's arm jerked violently as he pulled the trigger and the shot went wide, ploughing in the dirt of the corral over by the wall of the store.

'Damn!' This was going to be much harder than it looked.

'Think of the gun as an extension of yourself. If you're inclined to shake support your gunhand with your other hand. That's better.'

The next four shots all missed but the fifth was close, hitting the wall under the tin can. Polly reloaded the gun for him. The next bullet struck the can, the following one missed, and the final four all hit their targets, sending each can flying into the air.

Grant let out a cry of triumph.

'There, it's not too difficult, is it?' said Polly.

'Not when I have a good teacher like you.'

'You should practise each day.'

Grant agreed.

'And Grant, don't try to pick a fight with Vince. He's been around guns all his life. He'll probably beat you. But if you show him you can defend yourself, somehow I doubt he'll want to go up against you. Oh, here's Mr Kent,' Polly added as the man rode into the yard.

'Problem solved,' he said to Grant as he swung down from his horse. His eyes narrowed as he saw the gun and the targets. 'Polly, what's going on?'

'Vince beat Lonnie up. He's inside. Iris is looking after him.'

'Dammit! Iris isn't hurt, is she?'

'No,' Polly reassured him. 'She was frightened but more for Lonnie than herself. Unfortunately Vince was off Brad's leash.'

'I'll go and see her.'

'Can Lonnie stay here?' Grant asked anxiously. 'Till he's better?'

'Of course he can.' Kent frowned at Grant and the gun he wore. 'You ain't planning on doing anything foolish I hope?'

'No, sir.'

But Grant hoped Vincent would try something foolish with him. And be taught a much-needed lesson. Perhaps he could find a way to make sure that happened.

CHAPTER TWELVE

Grant didn't want to go back to the farm and leave Lonnie behind. At the same time he could do nothing for him. His brother was being well looked after by Iris. So he picked up some more supplies, then went over to the saloon to say goodbye to Polly. She kissed him long and hard, after which he truly didn't want to leave Salt Creek.

It was a lonely ride back to the farm. He didn't really know how he felt beyond being overwhelmingly angry and upset over Lonnie. How dare Vincent behave like he had, just because he was a rich rancher's son and Lonnie was an inexperienced sodbuster.

Grant no longer thought that what had happened was any of his fault. They had the right to be out here on Jethro's land. It was theirs. And Lonnie had the right to talk to Iris, to court her, especially as she said she had no feelings for Vincent. Likely Polly was correct when she said Vincent had no feelings for Iris either but only wanted her because she didn't want him.

It was all very well for Mr Kent to tell Grant not to

act rashly. Grant wanted to do something to stop Vincent, rash or not.

Somehow he wasn't at all surprised to see McGrath, Vincent and some of the Circle M hands gathered at the farm when he got home. He fingered the Colt on his hip. He probably couldn't beat any one of them, let alone all of them, to the draw or shoot well enough to hit his target but right then he wouldn't have minded trying.

He kicked the horse into a gallop and crossed the creek, splashing through the water, and came to a halt by McGrath, who turned in the saddle to face him. Beyond him, Brad Howden was standing by his own animal, an awkward look on his face.

Grant didn't wait for McGrath to greet him.

'What are you doing here?' He glared round him. 'Your men are causing damage to my property. I'd be obliged if you'd stop them. And then leave.'

'Now, now, there's no need for that—'

'I asked, Mr McGrath, what you're doing here?'

McGrath's face reddened with anger.

Go for your gun, Grant said to himself, his heart pounding, go on.

But he didn't. With a deep breath the rancher said:

'I received a report that some of my cattle had been rustled and were seen down here by the creek on your land.'

Thank God he and Lonnie had gone into Salt Creek and secured Mr Kent's help. Thank God the cattle were no longer here. He couldn't help but glance at the rope secured to the cantle of McGrath's saddle.

'Really? Well,' he shrugged, 'I can't see any cattle, can you? Perhaps your informant,' he looked at Vincent and smirked, 'was mistaken?' He was aware of Howden quickly hiding a smile.

It was obvious from Vincent's face that this was another one of his schemes that had gone awry. Good. But it was worrying that Morgan McGrath had been so willing to believe and act on the report; especially when he must have known how unlikely it was that Grant and Lonnie would be capable of rustling twenty or so longhorns, or willing to do so, particularly when they had been warned of the consequences.

'Yeah I guess,' McGrath admitted not too pleasantly. 'Brad, get everyone ready to ride out. Sorry to have troubled you.'

Grant watched the men ride away. Only Howden looked back, tipping his hat to Grant, making the boy think the foreman was only too aware that Vincent had left the cattle here and that he didn't approve.

'Home sweet home, boys!' Fletcher dismounted and stretched. It had been a long, hot ride but now they were here in the mountains, safe for a while. 'Ricky, gather up some wood, let's get a fire goin'. Have something to eat.'

'Yeah,' Reece agreed. 'I'm starving.'

Ricky got off his horse and walked away to do as he was told, thinking he always had to do the hard work.

All three were glad to have reached the hide out they used when in this part of the country. Not that it was much of a place. Just a shack that must once have belonged to an unsuccessful miner. It was half-ruined, with the door hanging off its hinges, its one window unshuttered and holes in the walls. But it did provide a certain amount of shelter and warmth and they could store tinned food inside, while there was a lean-to at the back for their horses. It was also in an ideal spot, remote, half-way up the mountain slope, well hidden by trees, with no other buildings nearby. They could stay here, knowing no one from the Circle M, or any of the other ranches in the area, would come by and find them.

Fletcher and Reece unsaddled the three horses, letting them roam free to feed on the grass. While they waited for Ricky to start up the stove and make coffee and open some tins of beef, they sat on the doorstep, enjoying the rest and the warmth of the early evening.

As he came by with an armful of wood, Ricky stopped.

'I don't see why we couldn't've stopped in Salt Creek and had a drink at The Steer's Horns.' It was the umpteenth time he'd complained about the same thing, making Reece want to hit him. 'I wanted a beer. There ain't no beer here. You ain't punishing me for what happened in Mexico, are you? You are, ain't you?'

'Like I told you,' Fletcher said patiently. 'Salt Creek is too small. Everyone knows us there.'

'As if any one of 'em would dare do a thing about us,' Ricky muttered. 'We could deal with any trouble.'

'Why cause trouble when there's no need?' Reece said.

'It's safer in Tucson,' Fletcher agreed. 'People are always coming and goin' there. No one knows us. And there's more to do as well. Look at what The Steer's Horns has to offer. Nothing. We go to Tucson we can find any manner of entertainment.'

'We've gotta get there first.'

Determined to ignore the boy's whining, Reece said, 'So, Pete, what's the plan?'

'First we've gotta find out where some of old McGrath's cattle are being kept. We need at least thirty head to make it worthwhile. Then we drive 'em off.' Fletcher looked at Reece and grinned. 'Neither should be difficult.'

Reece grinned back. 'It never is. Hey, Ricky, that coffee ready yet?'

Lonnie rolled over in bed and with a little groan opened his eyes. Where was he? Why did he hurt so much? There didn't seem to be one part of his body that didn't ache. He certainly wasn't at the farm. This bed was much more comfortable than the one he had to share with Grant. He rolled back and saw Iris Kent sitting on a chair nearby, leaning forward anxiously. Iris!

As she saw he was awake she put aside a piece of sewing and stood up, came over to him.

'Lonnie, dear, how do you feel?'

'Awful,' he said in a croaky voice.

'Here.' Iris raised his head a little and put a glass of water to his lips. 'Just a sip or two. Do you remember what happened? Vince beat you up.'

'Oh yes,' Lonnie said darkly, collapsing back against the pillow. That was the reason for his aches and pains, the fact that one of his eyes was half-closed. 'Where's Grant?'

'It was thought best you stay here where I could look after you—'

Lonnie decided it was worth getting beaten up for that.

'—while Grant went back to the farm.'

'On his own?'

'Yes.'

'Does he know what Vincent did?'

'Of course he does. Lonnie,' Iris paused then spoke in a rush, 'Grant has bought a gun. And Polly, that's the girl who works at the saloon, taught him to shoot it.'

'Oh God!' It seemed as if Lonnie's worst dreams might still be coming true: Grant and a gun!

'He's good too,' Iris added, making Lonnie feel worse.

'I'd better go on out and stop him from doing whatever he has in mind.'

As Lonnie tried to sit up, Iris pushed him back down, for which he was thankful as the room started to spin round.

'Don't be silly. You're not well enough to ride all that way. Grant will be OK. He's promised not to do anything silly.'

But then no one here knew that Grant's definition of silly might be different from theirs. Unfortunately Iris was right. He was in no fit state to ride to the rescue.

'Would you like some soup? There's some warming on the stove.'

'Yes, please.'

Lonnie watched Iris go, realizing he was falling in love with her; did love her. Hoped she could come to care for him. He thought she did. Before Vincent had come in and spoiled everything, he remembered being in the store with her, the pleasure he'd found in helping her tidy the shelves. How they hadn't needed words to show they were enjoying one another's company.

He sighed. How much better he'd like it if he could work in the store rather than on the farm. And not just because of Iris. But also because he knew he'd be much more at home doing that sort of work than digging the land or working with animals.

But how to tell Grant that? Lonnie didn't want to let him down. And until some more of the family arrived out here to help, which wasn't likely to be any time real soon, no one except their mother wanting to leave New York, Grant couldn't manage by himself. And now he was out there, alone, with a gun! Lonnie decided that the sooner he was up and about and could ride out to the farm again the better. Even if it meant leaving Iris.

Lonnie wasn't the only Cunningham brother dreaming of a girl. Grant lay in bed that night thinking about Polly.

Of course he knew what she was and how she made a living but that didn't matter. People couldn't always help what they were forced to do in order to live. Especially on the frontier where sometimes life was harsh. She'd been only too willing to help him, and Lonnie, so who was he to judge her and what she did?

Just before falling asleep he wondered if Polly was thinking of him too and hoped so.

CHAPTER THIRTEEN

Brad Howden was in a bad mood; no, not so much bad, he thought, but unhappy. Life at the Circle M was becoming impossible. The younger cowboys took little notice of him, preferring to spend their free time with Vincent. Giggling and plotting with him. Something had happened in Salt Creek the day before yesterday, something to do with the Cunningham brothers, but those involved fell silent when they saw their foreman and it was no use asking any of them what had gone on for none would dare tell tales about Vincent.

McGrath was going around like a bear with a sore head and Vincent was going around like a bear with a sore everything. All because the Cunninghams had arrived to take over their uncle's farm, which they were perfectly within their rights to do.

The atmosphere was getting Howden down and he decided to leave it all behind for a while and act like a proper foreman again, like the proper cowboy he once was and not like Vincent's nursemaid. He'd ride out and make sure there was still grass enough for the cattle where they were or whether he should start ordering them moved.

It was a lovely morning, not quite as hot as it had been the last few days, a breeze coming off the mountain and making it pleasant. There was even the hint of rain in the gathering clouds on the far horizon, although it was doubtful it would come to anything.

As he rode along, Howden remembered how it had been in the old days when it was just him and Morgan McGrath working together, building the place up, facing hazards square on. They'd been good days, the work hard, the days long but McGrath had been a father to him and they got along well. Why couldn't it be like it was? But Howden knew it hadn't been the same for years, not since Vincent grew old enough to become troublesome, and now would never be so again; that there was no going back.

Things had been getting worse for quite a while and the arrival of the two Cunningham brothers was somehow bringing it all to a head. Grant Cunningham had bested Vincent and Vincent was not about to forget or forgive, or forget that Howden had been a witness. It was all boiling up for trouble.

Not for the first time in the past few days he wondered what he was going to do. He didn't want to let McGrath down, the man had been good to him, but why should he stay at a place where he wasn't happy and where not only did Vincent not give him the respect he and his position deserved but was succeeding in turning some of the other hands against him too? And if push came to shove McGrath would naturally support his son over his foreman.

Perhaps he should just leave . . . .

After about an hour's ride Howden reached the first slopes of the foothills. Some thirty head had been driven up here a couple of weeks ago. They should be in the next valley.

'If our information is right, the cattle should be in the meadow beyond those rocks.' Fletcher pointed to a high stand of boulders on the side of a bare hill. He pulled his horse to a halt and took a drink from his canteen.

'How many?' Reece asked.

'About thirty head. Easy enough for us to handle.'

'Then we'll be on our way to Tucson, right?' Ricky said, thinking about the saloons and the girls.

'Right,' Fletcher agreed with a grin, thinking much the same. 'We'll probably get there before McGrath even realizes his cattle are missing.'

'Even if he does and sends men after us we'll be ready for 'em.' Ricky eased his gun in its holster.

None of them was worried. Cowboys would be no match for them.

They rode on and when they rounded the rocks they saw the information was right. In the meadow beyond were some thirty head of cattle, sleek and fat.

'By the looks of the grass we've made it just in time,' Fletcher said. 'It won't be long before some of McGrath's hands come up here to drive the beeves on to higher ground. Oh dear.' He grinned. 'When that happens the cattle will already be sold in Tucson, the brand altered and they'll be on their way to the reservation!'

*

Grant spent the morning planting vegetables, for which he'd spent all of the day before clearing a patch of ground. Digging the ground had been hard work, with the sun beating down on his head, and planting the vegetables wasn't much better, but he knew it was important for him and Lonnie to feed themselves as much as possible. They couldn't keep relying on Mr Kent's generosity to supply tinned food. Mr Kent had, after all, also supplied the seed potatoes and seeds for tomatoes and onions. The man had said they should think about buying a milk cow and Polly had promised to come out and show them how to milk it.

As he watered the ground where he'd planted the vegetables, Grant thought it was a good job they'd found people in Salt Creek willing to help them by loaning them money and providing advice. *Mr Hobson's First Class Manual* was only satisfactory up to a point and the money they'd brought out with them from New York only just about covered essentials.

The previous night he'd written a letter to his mother. The next time he went into Salt Creek he'd ask Mr Kent to give it to a carter going to the stage-coach halt. In it he hadn't said anything about the McGraths or any trouble but he had mentioned how difficult everything was and how he hoped she could see her way to sending out more money so they could pay their already considerable debts!

There! That was everything done. He was pleased with himself. The vegetables were planted in neat rows. Would hopefully soon start growing.

Thinking of the McGraths, Grant had earlier gathered up some large pebbles from the creekbed. Now he placed them on a boulder, took up a position some way away and drew the gun he had decided to wear all the time. He aimed and fired. Five times. Four hits and a near miss.

As he was a good shot perhaps he should take the gun and go hunting. He was well aware that shooting at a rock or a tin can was completely different from shooting an animal but it wasn't as though he'd be doing it for fun or sport; it would be to eat. With a revolver he'd only be able to shoot something small like a rabbit and he'd probably have to get quite close to it. He might not succeed, he wasn't sure he could even kill an animal, but at least he could try.

With a last look round, he mounted the horse and headed out for the mountain where Mr Kent said game was to be found all year round.

Howden heard the cattle before he saw them. Heard them bawling. What was wrong? His first thought was wolves or even a mountain lion, although they didn't often come this low down, especially during the day. Then almost at the same time he caught the sound of a man's shout.

Rustlers! It had to be. None of the cowboys was up here.

Angrily he drew his rifle from its scabbard and urged his horse forward. Slowly. Not knowing how many men were involved he wasn't going to take any chances. He intended to reach the rocks and there dismount and climb amongst them. Find out what the situation was and if it favoured him shoot at the rustlers from safety.

He didn't make it.

He was almost there when the first of the cattle appeared coming towards him, calmer now because the men driving them knew what they were doing. Three men. Howden recognized them. The Fletchers and Reece. Everyone in Salt Creek thought they were rustlers but there was never any evidence to prove it. Until now.

As he saw the rustlers they saw him.

'Hey!' Reece yelled. 'Look out!'

'Get him!'

Cursing, Howden raised his rifle. So did Pete and Ricky.

Grant was almost at the spot where Jethro had been ambushed when several shots rang out. He jumped, his heart beating violently, fearing that the same fate was about to befall him.

Then he realized the shots were coming from some way away. On the other side of the trees. Without thinking he turned his horse's head in that direction and gigged it forward. As he did so the firing stopped.

CHAPTER FOURTEEN

Grant hadn't gone very far when, emerging from a thicket of cypress trees, he was almost knocked off his horse by a group of fast-running cattle. The horse skittered away, nearly unseating him. As he struggled to control the animal and stay in the saddle, he heard a shout.

'There's another of 'em!'

More shots rang out. And this time they *were* aimed at him. When one bullet whined past his ear he yelped in surprise and half-fell, half-dived off the horse to land in the undergrowth. By the time he'd recovered enough from his fright to stand up and make a grab for his gun, both cattle and the men shooting at him were at the bottom of the hill and out of range.

'Damn!'

He dusted himself down, feeling annoyed with himself for the way he'd reacted; he hadn't even drawn his gun let alone got a shot off.

Suddenly movement at the top of the slope caught

his eye. Not more shooters! Heart missing a beat he swung round. And saw only a horse waiting by some rocks. What was it doing there? Did it belong to whoever those men had been shooting at? He decided he'd better go and find out.

Grant hurried up the slope, dragging his horse after him. His heart began to beat fast as he saw a dark shape lying on the ground. Was he about to see his first-ever dead man? He swallowed hard against the thought and breathed a sigh of relief when, as he got closer, the man sat up, clutching at his left arm. Grant recognized him – Brad Howden, the Circle M foreman. He also saw there was blood on the man's sleeve.

'Are you wounded?' he asked. 'Have you been shot?'

'Yeah,' Howden said with a little grimace. 'Help me, will you?'

'Of course.'

'Get my canteen.'

Grant did so and when he turned back saw Howden had torn away his shirt sleeve. He swallowed again. Howden took the canteen from him and poured some water over the sleeve. With it he wiped away the blood.

'Is the bullet still in your arm?'

'No.'

'Are you sure?'

Howden laughed. 'Yeah, look. The bullet grazed my arm from front to back. It's a deep graze and it stings like hell but that's all.'

'It's still bleeding.' Grant couldn't quite figure out

how the man could be so unconcerned. He was sure that if he'd been shot, even if it had only been a graze – and to him the wound looked deep and nasty – he would be demanding to visit a doctor or be scared he'd bleed to death.

'It'll be OK once I wrap a strip of my shirt round it.' Howden tore the sleeve into pieces. 'Tie it for me. Then I can be on my way after those bastards.'

Grant came to a halt and gaped.

'After them? You mean you're going after them? On your own?'

'That's right,' Howden said with an amused glint in his eyes. 'Once you've bandaged me up, that is.'

'But you can't.' Grant knelt down by the man. 'You're hurt. You need the wound treated.'

'I told you I'll be OK. I've been hurt worse than this. Tie it tightly but not too tight.'

'Weren't there three men?'

'Yeah.'

'That makes it three against one. Shouldn't you fetch help before you go chasing them?'

'Be too late. By the time I reach the ranch and then come back out here, they'll be long gone.'

'Even though they're driving cattle?'

'Afraid so. And this land has numerous places in which they can hide. They've struck us before and always gotten away with it. This is my chance to catch 'em and stop 'em.'

'Can you, though? They've already shot you.'

'That's only because I wasn't ready for 'em. I will be ready next time.'

Grant sighed unhappily. 'In that case, as you're so

determined, I'd better go with you.'

'You?' Howden sounded surprised. 'It ain't your fight. There's no need. Especially after the way the McGraths have treated you.'

'You're not the McGraths. You're especially not Vincent.'

'That I ain't.'

Grant finished bandaging the man's arm and helped him to his feet.

'Well then?'

'I don't want to be responsible for getting you hurt.'

'I can look after myself.'

'So I see.' Although Howden glanced at the gun on Grant's hip, he didn't sound too sure.

'And it's my decision, not yours.'

'Well, if I am to catch up with the Fletchers there's no time to argue. But just be careful and if I say duck you duck, understand?'

'Yes, sir.'

Grant couldn't understand why he was doing this, although doubtless Lonnie would accuse him of wanting some foolish excitement. But he could hardly let the foreman go after the rustlers on his own. It would be neither right nor fair. He caught up both horses and helped Howden into the saddle.

As they set off down the hill, he said, 'You know who those men are?'

'Yeah. Pete and Ricky Fletcher and their cohort, George Reece. They've been hanging around Salt Creek off and on for several months now. Always got money to spend without doing any work to earn it.'

'That doesn't make them rustlers.'

'Good chance of it. And now I've got proof.' Howden glanced across at Grant. 'Proof to act I mean. Proof to handle this situation myself.'

Grant nodded, knowing the man intended to shoot them or capture them so they could be strung up.

'If you can't cope with that then you'd better go on back to your farm.'

'I can cope,' Grant said, hoping he could. 'Mr Howden?'

'Yeah?'

'Did you know Vincent beat up my brother?'

Howden glanced sharply at him.

'No. I wondered where Lonnie was. You two always seem to be together. I also thought Vince and his friends had been up to something they didn't want me or Mr McGrath to know about. Vince has been strutting around the last couple of days like he's pleased with himself, which is never a good sign. Is Lonnie all right?'

'I think so. I had to leave him in Salt Creek. Iris Kent is looking after him.'

Howden shook his head. 'I'm afraid there's something wrong with Vince. He's always been spoiled by his father, so much so I don't think he ever learnt right from wrong.'

'Would his father approve if he knew what he'd done?'

'Probably not. But I don't suppose he'd do anything.'

'Why not?'

'Because Mr McGrath loves his son even while he disapproves of him.' Howden looked across at the boy and with a little sigh, went on, 'You know, Grant, despite all his wealth and position Mr McGrath is a lonely and disappointed man. He's worked hard to build up the Circle M, he's proud of it and everything he's achieved, but he knows full well that when he dies and it passes on to his son, Vince will never be able to run it efficiently. Or willingly. The only things Vince cares about is himself and spending money. Once he gets his hands on the ranch he'll either sell it or ruin it. Only thing is I won't be around to see either one. I shall be long gone by then.'

Grant was puzzled. 'If you don't like Vincent and you won't want to stay on once his father dies, then why are you risking your life for the ranch?'

'Because right now I'm its foreman. It's my job.'

Soon they reached the bottom of the hill. The trail was easy to follow. It snaked to the left and crossed a meadow into more trees and rocks.

'Heading for Tucson,' Howden said. 'I've long suspected our cattle are taken there and end up feeding the reservation Apaches.'

'Will we be able to catch up?'

'I hope so. I doubt Fletcher will think anyone is coming after them. They probably believed they killed me.'

'Why?'

'Because otherwise they'd have come back to finish the job.'

'Oh.' Life sure was cheap out here.

Howden was right about catching up. The cattle were on the far side of the trees, meandering along towards another slope that led down to the desert floor.

'Got 'em.' Howden was pleased because it was obvious the rustlers were certain they were safe, were taking no precautions. He turned to look at Grant. 'You sure about this?'

Of course Grant wasn't sure. He didn't want to risk his life for Circle M cattle; unlike Howden he didn't even work for the ranch. He didn't want to get shot and wounded, or killed. He didn't want to shoot and wound, or kill, anyone else. But he was here now. There was no going back. He nodded.

'Good.' Howden drew his rifle from its scabbard. 'Let's go.'

CHAPTER FIFTEEN

Lonnie sat with Iris Kent and Polly Summers in chairs pulled up in the shade cast by the rear wall of the saloon. The Steer's Horns was nearly empty at this time of day, so Nathon didn't need Polly's help. On a little table in front of them were cool beers.

Lonnie was as shocked as Grant that Iris should speak to a saloon girl and very shocked that she should drink beer. But he loved her too much to criticize her out loud. And, like Grant, he was quickly coming to realize that many things were different out here from how they were in New York and if he was going to stay he had to accept them.

He felt better this afternoon, having spent the day before in bed and then sleeping the night away. Everything still hurt and he was stiff all over but at least he could now walk without help and his head was clear.

'I'll have to go back to the farm soon,' he said reluctantly, drinking some of his beer.

'Oh, do you have to?' Iris asked.

'I don't want to,' Lonnie admitted. He'd much sooner stay here with Iris. 'But I'd better.'

Goodness knew what was happening. He was scared Vincent might be up to more of his tricks or that Grant might be working himself up to go after Vincent, call him out. Not that Lonnie could stop Grant if he decided to do something like that.

'Do you feel well enough?' Iris said. 'You don't want to do yourself any hurt.'

'I'm OK.'

Polly said, 'You can't go now, it's much too hot. Those rain-clouds never came to anything and it'll be baking out on the desert floor. You'll have to wait till later on. I shouldn't fret too much, Lonnie; after what he did I expect Vince is lying low, don't you think so, Iris? Vince ain't the bravest of young men and he'll be scared either his pa will find out what he did and tick him off or that you and Grant will go after him.'

'That's right,' Iris added with a little nod. 'And it's a busy time out on the ranch with the cattle having to be moved further into the hills. As foreman, Brad Howden gives orders for that sort of thing but Vince likes to be there too so he can pretend he's in charge. Of course, everyone's aware he hasn't the least idea over what he's doing.'

She and Polly exchanged a smile. Both girls knew Vincent McGrath wasn't worth much.

'And surely even Grant can't get into any trouble in a couple of days.'

'Polly, you don't know Grant!'

'And I don't think you ought to ride yet,' Iris said, wanting Lonnie to stay in town.

Lonnie had been dreading the thought of getting

on a horse again. He wasn't a very good rider, rarely having ridden in New York, and he was fearful of getting bumped about or even falling off and bruising his bruises.

'How else am I going to reach the farm?'

'You'll have to go in a buckboard.'

'How can I? I'm sure Mr Brookmeyer won't let me borrow another one, seeing as what happened to his last one. Even if I had the money to pay for it, which I don't.'

'Don't worry,' Polly told him. 'The saloon has its own buckboard and I expect Nathon will let me borrow it. I can take you out there and then drive it back.'

That would give her the chance to see Grant again, something she wanted to do. And she wouldn't wear her low-cut dress, so hopefully Grant would see she wasn't just a saloon girl, would like her for herself.

'On your own?'

'Yeah, of course,' Polly laughed. 'I came here from Texas all by myself. I've been handling horses since I was a child.' And maybe if they didn't get out there too quickly, it would be too late for her to drive back to town and she would have to stay the night at the farm.

She looked from one to the other of them. She was aware that Lonnie would much rather it was Iris who took him. But Nathon probably wouldn't want to let anyone else but Polly drive the buckboard and Mr Kent probably wouldn't want Iris coming home all that way alone, especially when it might be dark before she reached Salt Creek. Still, she thought with a little smile, she could leave them together for a while now.

She stood up and collected the beer-glasses.

'I'll go and speak to Nathon and get us some more beer. I won't be long.' She winked at Lonnie to let him know she'd take as long as she could and was amused at how red he went.

Vincent got up out of the armchair, walked to the bookshelf and glanced at the books. Finding nothing he wanted to read he flung himself back into the chair, slouching, a petulant scowl on his face.

McGrath looked up from his desk where he was trying to balance the accounts.

'For goodness sake, Vince, whatever is the matter with you? I'm working on something important here and your fidgeting keeps making me lose my place and I have to start all over again.' He paused to see if his son apologized. Needless to say Vincent didn't do so. McGrath sighed. 'If you can't sit still go outside and see if Brad has got any work for you to do.'

At any other time Vincent might have said something about objecting to doing what a mere foreman told him but he could tell his father wasn't in the mood. With his own sigh he stood up again and went out, making sure he slammed the door behind him.

McGrath stared after him. Sometimes Vincent was quite impossible.

Hands in his pockets, feeling bored, Vincent left the house and wandered slowly down to the corral where a few of the hands were sitting out the hottest part of the afternoon mending some harness. Vincent had no intention of helping with that sort of mundane work and he was glad he could see no sign of Howden.

The few young cowboys who liked to hang around with Vincent were nowhere to be seen either. Vincent had the idea that they thought he'd gone too far in beating up Lonnie Cunningham and were not only keeping out of his way but were also scared Howden would find out and dismiss them. So much for them! He could do without cowards like that and their friendship.

He stared at the men, wondering if he could start ordering them around but Howden had obviously given out his own orders before he left to do whatever he was doing. They might refuse to take any notice of him. In most cases the men were experienced cowboys and didn't need to be told what to do by anyone. In the same way his father didn't need help with the paperwork, said he could do it much quicker on his own, so Vincent had given up asking if he could learn any of the business. Not that he was much interested anyway.

In his heart he knew he had no real role around the Circle M. And while he told himself he wasn't concerned about the ranch it was yet another source of dissatisfaction.

He didn't even dare ride into Salt Creek, especially on his own, in case anyone there challenged him over beating up Lonnie Cunningham. Instead he turned to go back to the house. A few days ago he'd bought a bottle of whiskey. Some of it was left. He'd finish it up.

*

When Polly came out of the saloon carrying three beers, she was exasperated to see Lonnie and Iris were still sitting in the same chairs as when she'd left them. Had Lonnie taken the chance to kiss the girl? Not if the sulky look on Iris's face was anything to go by!

Did Lonnie think that as a respectable girl Iris wouldn't want to be kissed? If so he had a lot to learn about girls, respectable or not, and if she had the chance Polly determined to let him in on a few facts of life when she drove him out to the farm. And, of course, Iris was too respectable to kiss him first. Perhaps Polly should have a word with her as well!

'It's OK,' she said putting down the beers. 'Nathon says we can borrow the buckboard. We'll go as soon as it starts to cool down.'

CHAPTER SIXTEEN

Heart in his mouth, Grant followed Howden out of the trees. Once they were clear the foreman kicked his horse into a gallop. The cattle weren't far ahead and it didn't seem any time at all before they had caught up to them.

One rustler was leading the drive, another was on the far side and the third, the youngest, rode at the rear. Ricky Fletcher was the first to realize the danger. He turned in his saddle and let out a yell of surprise and fright.

Howden didn't hesitate. He raised his rifle and fired. The bullet struck Ricky in the chest, knocking him out of the saddle. He fell on his back, tried to get up and then collapsed.

Grant thought the young man was dead and he swallowed hard on both his fear and excitement. Then he and Howden were past him, among the herd. And Fletcher and Reece were returning the fire.

The cattle were already spooked and now took it into their heads to run.

'Watch out!' Howden yelled to Grant above the

cattle's bawling and the dust raised by their pounding hoofs. 'Stay on your horse whatever you do.'

Grant saw the sense of that and he clung to reins and saddle horn, forgetting all about the fact that he was meant to be shooting rustlers.

At the front of the stampede the cattle were pouring all round Fletcher, leaving him with little choice but to turn his horse and go along with them. Leaving Reece alone. He'd seen Ricky go down and not get up again. Was he dead? Even if Ricky was only wounded, Fletcher didn't give much for his brother's chances, not once he fell into Circle M hands. Morgan McGrath had the reputation for hanging rustlers mercilessly. He wanted to go back for his brother but at the moment he could do nothing about either Reece or Ricky, all he could do was concentrate on saving his own hide.

Seeing what was happening, that he was on his own, Reece cursed wildly and sent his horse towards a nearby group of rocks. As he reached their safety he dismounted and grabbed hold of rifle and revolver. He ducked down behind the boulders and started to shoot at the ranch foreman and the kid who was with him. Perhaps, with a lucky shot or two, he could get out of this . . . .

Howden wanted to go after Fletcher, the leader of the gang, but to do that he had to get by Reece and he didn't want to leave Grant alone to handle the man. Grant was willing enough but he was inexperienced and only had a revolver. Capturing or killing Fletcher wasn't worth getting Grant killed.

The cattle were gone by now, heading for the

desert, and through the dust Howden galloped up to Grant.

'Get off your horse,' he ordered. He flung himself off his own animal and lay down on the ground, not giving Reece much of a target.

Grant soon did the same when he felt a bullet pluck at the sleeve of his shirt.

'Go to the right, I'll go to the left.' Howden raised himself and ran in a crouch towards the rocks, shooting as he went, drawing Reece's fire.

Grant knew he should do what Howden said but for some reason his legs wouldn't move properly. They felt so wobbly he didn't think they would support him. So he contented himself with firing at the rocks from where he was, even though he was too far away to do any damage; and hoped Howden wouldn't accuse him of being a coward.

From his hiding-place Reece was cursing and shouting. He would never have believed Fletcher would leave him alone like he had. He thought they were pals.

Not that there was a great deal Fletcher could do. By the time he disentangled himself from the stampede he was a mile or more away. More rocks stood near to where he had come to a halt and leaving his horse he climbed amongst them so he could see what was happening.

Ricky hadn't moved. He was dead for sure. And the two bastards were closing in on Reece.

He could have ridden back but he knew that by the time he got there it would be all over. One way or the other. He'd risk being shot or caught for nothing. At least that was what he told himself, although he probably would have tried had it been Ricky in the rocks and Reece dead.

Hell! How had it all gone so very wrong? He was certain they'd killed the ranch foreman – but he should have gone back to make absolutely certain, then they wouldn't be in this fix. And where the hell had that kid come from? Who was he?

Howden inched closer to the rocks. Reece was firing at him, obviously believing Grant didn't pose much of a threat. When Howden thought he was close enough he paused, got to one knee and began to fire quickly and steadily, keeping Reece pinned down.

One of the bullets ricocheted off a boulder, sending chippings flying everywhere. Suddenly Reece gave a little cry. With one hand pawing at his left eye, which must have been struck by a sliver of rock, he rose to his feet. His body was exposed, making a good target. He must have realized his danger for his other hand came up, lifting his Colt. He was too late.

Howden aimed, pulled the trigger. Didn't miss.

With another cry, Reece was knocked sideways. He fell among the rocks and didn't get up.

'Stay where you are,' Howden called to Grant. 'It might be a trick.' Although he didn't think so. Cautiously he stood up and even more cautiously approached the rocks, gun ready to fire again.

He didn't need to worry. Reece was propped up in the boulders and he was clearly dead.

'OK, Grant.'

Somewhat unsteadily Grant walked towards

Howden. He didn't particularly want to look at Reece, a dead body, but somehow he felt he must. He had after all been part of the shoot-out; if a rather ineffectual part. And it could have been his bullet which struck the man, even though he knew it wasn't. When he looked he thought what an awful lot of blood there was and, worse, a lot of damage to the man's face.

From his vantage point, Fletcher watched the two men stare down at Reece. He too was clearly dead. What was he going to do? His brother was dead. So was his friend. Both shot by that bastard, Brad Howden. And the cattle were gone, strung out from here to kingdom come. Well, the first thing to do was tell Vince McGrath, ask for his help. Because the second thing was to avenge himself on Howden and the kid. Grieving over Ricky could come later. On unsteady legs he climbed down from the rocks, mounted his horse and kicked it into a flat-out gallop.

'Is he dead?' Grant asked, thinking it was a stupid question because it was obvious Reece was dead even to someone who'd never seen a corpse before.

'Yeah.' Howden glanced at him. 'You OK 'bout this?'

Grant nodded. 'It's just I've never seen . . .' he began, before stumbling away to be violently sick.

Howden took no notice. He glanced up to where Ricky Fletcher hadn't moved. Leaving Grant alone to recover he climbed the hillside to make sure the boy was dead. When he got back, Grant, somewhat shamefaced, apologized.

'It's all right,' Howden told him. 'Those two ain't the first men I've killed but taking another's life even when they're trying to take yours ain't something to accept lightly. But, Grant, either one would have shot you given the chance and I doubt they'd have thought much about it.'

'Where's the other one gone?' Grant glanced over his shoulder, hoping the third rustler wasn't sneaking up on them.

'I don't know. But don't worry, he's long gone. And so are the cattle.' A spiral of dust in the distance was all there was to be seen of the steers.

'What are you going to do?'

'I'll have to go back to the ranch, let Mr McGrath know what's happened. Get some of the boys to come out here to see if we can recover the cattle and bury these two.'

'Aren't you taking them to Salt Creek?'

'No. Ain't nowhere to bury 'em there, is there?'

Miserably Grant shook his head.

'Hey.' Howden slapped his shoulder. 'You did a good job.'

'Did I?'

'Sure. Look, why don't you go on back to the farm? Rest up. I'll come by either later on today or tomorrow morning to see how you are. OK?'

'Yes.' Grant didn't really want to be left by himself but he didn't want Howden to think badly of him and besides the foreman had a job to do.

Howden waited until Grant had mounted his horse and was heading towards the mountain before riding away. Grant turned in the saddle to watch him go. He'd never felt more lonely. Two men had been shot dead here today and although he hadn't killed either one he'd had a hand in it. How did he feel? Grant didn't know. It was all very well for Howden to say the two men were shooting at them. Even so . . .

And yet before coming out here Grant had known that shoot-outs happened. Not perhaps with the frequency written about in dime novels but they took place nevertheless and the result was that men were killed.

But, oh hell, what was Lonnie going to say when he found out?

CHAPTER SEVENTEEN

Vincent was half-way back to the house when pounding hoofbeats from the direction of the mountains stopped him. A horse and rider was approaching fast. What had happened? Was it Howden having discovered the cattle had gone? Vincent grinned but the smile died on his face as he recognized the rider. Pete Fletcher! What the hell did he think he was doing coming here when someone might see him? Anyway he should be on his way to Tucson by now. What did he want? What had gone wrong?

Vincent glanced round. Luckily the few hands about the place were occupied with what they were doing. Hadn't spotted the rider or, if they had, hadn't taken any notice.

Quickly he hurried forward, intercepting Fletcher before he got any closer. He held up a hand to stop the man. With a curse, Fletcher pulled his horse to a halt. Both horse and rider were covered with sweat, both wild-eyed.

'What the hell do you think you're up to? Coming

here. You might be seen.' Vincent's voice rose to a shout. Then he saw Fletcher's face. It was twisted with pain and fury. Vincent wisely stepped back out of the way.

Fletcher swung down from the saddle.

'Reece and Ricky are dead! Howden shot them.'

'What?'

'And the cattle are gone too.'

'Oh damn.' There went Vincent's profit! Wisely he decided not to mention that but to act as if upset over Ricky and Reece. 'God, Pete, I'm sorry. How did it happen?'

'I dunno. We found the cattle where you told us they'd be. We were driving 'em out, like usual, when that sonofabitch, Howden, appeared out of nowhere.'

'Didn't you shoot him?' There were three rustlers against one foreman. They should have been able to handle Howden. But Vincent didn't like to point that out.

'I thought we had,' Fletcher said bitterly. 'But he came after us. Ambushed us. And he had help.'

'Help? Who?'

'Some kid I ain't never seen before. About twenty. Tall, with dark hair.'

'Oh hell! Grant Cunningham. I bet it was.'

'Does he work here?'

'No.' Vincent glanced round again. 'We'd better go somewhere where we can see to your horse and where we won't be spotted. Then I'll tell you all about Mr Damn Grant Cunningham! And decide what the hell we're going to do about him.'

*

Brad Howden rode home satisfied with his afternoon's work. Two rustlers dead and with help the cattle could soon be rounded up. He wished he'd been able to capture or kill Pete Fletcher but with the other gang members dead there would be no way he could cause any more trouble. He hoped Grant Cunningham would be all right. But if the boy wanted to make a life out here the sooner he learned first hand some of the harsh ways of the frontier the better.

It was quiet when he arrived back at the Circle M. The men would probably be resting in the heat of the afternoon. Howden decided that before rousting them out to go back into the hills with him he would rub down his horse, which had been hard-ridden for most of the day, and perhaps grab a bite to eat. There was no great rush. The two dead rustlers weren't going anywhere and the cattle would drift slowly along.

He dismounted and led his horse towards the barn. He was just about to enter the open door, looking forward to getting into the cool shade, when he heard Vincent say: '. . . kill the Cunningham kid and that damn bastard, Howden.'

Jesus! Howden came to a startled halt. He pushed his horse away and stepped closer, hand hovering over his gun. He peered round the door, unable to see anyone. Whoever Vincent was talking to they were hidden behind one of the wooden partitions. And who the hell *was* he talking to? Cautiously he moved forward. A horse stood, head hanging down in weariness, in one of the stalls. And Howden recognized it. It was the one Pete Fletcher had been riding. For a moment he thought he must be mistaken. Then he knew he wasn't. What was the horse doing here?

Heart thumping, Howden ducked down into another stall. The man Vincent was with moved into his line of sight. No. He wasn't mistaken. That was Pete Fletcher! And Vincent was deep in conversation with him.

Suddenly everything became clear. Howden had often wondered how the rustlers knew exactly where the cattle were grazing, especially when there were so many places in the hills and mountains where they could be. Now it was obvious. Vincent told them. Probably for a share of the profits.

The sad part, Howden thought, was that it wasn't difficult to believe it of Vincent. Instead it was easy to believe he was stealing from his father. God, it would break McGrath's heart. Damn Vincent to hell and back!

'Which one of the bastards first?' Fletcher asked.

'Have to be the kid. Howden is still out in the hills. He could be anywhere.'

'OK. So we kill the kid then come back here and lie in wait for Howden.'

'Yeah. Be good to teach both of them a lesson.'

'Where d'you think the kid is?'

'Gone back to his damn farm I expect,' Vincent said. 'He won't be hard to find. He's not real experienced at frontier life.'

'Right.'

While they were talking the men had been saddling up two horses. Now they led them past Howden and out into the open. Howden sent up a little prayer that neither would notice his own horse and realize he had in fact already arrived back at the ranch. But it seemed they didn't, for after a few moments he heard the sound of two horses galloping away.

He stood up. Now what did he do? One thing – he was on his own. Without proof, McGrath would never believe his own son was betraying him and he didn't want to let any of the other hands know; they wouldn't believe him either. And the second thing was – burying Ricky Fletcher and Reece could wait, so could rounding up the cattle. He had to warn Grant. He should never have left the boy alone. If anything happened to him, while it wouldn't be his fault he knew he would blame himself.

And he would be some way behind Vincent and Fletcher because his horse was in no fit state to be ridden all the way out to the farm. He would have to waste time saddling and bridling a fresh animal.

As he rode along Grant started to feel better, although he no longer had any desire to shoot anything, not even a rabbit for the pot.

He wasn't quite so happy when he realized he was lost, with no idea of where the farm was!

As he stopped his horse he saw nothing familiar and no landmarks nearby or in the distance that he recognized. This was stupid. He wanted to live on the frontier and he couldn't even find his way home. Thank goodness he was alone and no one needed to learn about this.

After his first panic subsided he knew he couldn't remain where he was. He rode slowly on, hoping he was going in the right direction. After a while he realized the slope of the mountain where Uncle Jethro had been shot was there in front of him. He must have been riding round in circles because it was some distance away yet but surely all he had to do was ride through the trees and he would come out on it somewhere. And once there he knew the way back. With a sigh of relief, he gigged his horse into a fast walk.

He was right. Beyond the trees was the mountain. He'd soon be home.

He had no more warning than his Uncle Jethro. One minute he was riding along, looking forward to getting back to the farm and having a cup of coffee and something to eat. The next, two men had jumped up from among the rocks in front of him. He didn't even have time to see who they were. Certainly had no time to do anything. Just knew they were holding rifles, and both guns were pointed at him.

Grant thought he let out a cry. But if he did the sound was drowned by the noise of both rifles being fired.

He felt a searing pain somewhere in his chest and his horse reared in fright.

Someone yelled: 'Got him!' Sounding triumphant.

Grant was knocked out of the saddle, finding himself falling, landing with a painful bump. The force of his fall sent him rolling on the ground. He crashed against a rock and unable to stop himself rolled further. Suddenly there was no ground under him and he was falling through space!

He shouted in terror and thumped against the mountainside. Somehow without really realizing what he did his hand snaked out, grabbing at the trunk of a small tree. His arm felt as if it was being wrenched out of its socket but at least he came to a halt. He scrabbled with his feet and other hand, trying to get a purchase on the earth. As he succeeded in doing so he saw the men who had tried to kill him arriving on the edge above.

Frightened, heart hammering, chest hurting, blood everywhere Grant pressed himself into the ground, keeping his head down, hoping he couldn't be seen.

Clearly he couldn't. Because he heard one of the men laugh and then Vincent McGrath said:

'You shot him, Pete, and now the silly bastard has rolled to the bottom of the mountain.'

'Yeah. He's dead for sure. It was as easy as when George and me killed that stupid old man . . .'

Pete Fletcher had killed Jethro! Grant's heart twisted with impotent anger.

'. . . Now for the other one.'

The men moved away and Grant allowed himself to breathe again. That was until he realized his situation. It was perilous to say the least. Here he was shot, perhaps badly wounded, lying on the side of the mountain, with no easy way to the top and a helluva long way to the bottom. And no one knew what had happened or where he was.

CHAPTER EIGHTEEN

'It's very quiet, ain't it?' Polly said as the pony pulled the buckboard across the creek.

It sure was. Lonnie bit his lip. No horse. No smoke from the wood stove. The door to the farm closed.

'I see Grant's planted some vegetables,' Polly said. 'In nice neat rows too.' She glanced at the boy's worried face. 'Don't fret, Lonnie, I expect he's gone out hunting. He did mention shooting something to cook and eat.'

'Yeah, maybe.'

As Polly pulled the pony to a stop in front of the house, the door opened. Their expectations swiftly changed to alarm as instead of Grant, Brad Howden emerged on to the porch.

'What are you doing here?' Lonnie demanded. 'Where's Grant?'

'Is he inside with you?' added Polly.

'No, Miss Polly, Grant ain't here.' Howden looked and sounded worried. 'And he should be by now.'

'Where is he?' Lonnie said again. 'What's happened?'

'I rather fear he's been shot.'

'What!' Polly cried.

Lonnie jumped down from the buckboard, ignoring the jolting this caused his aches and pains. With Polly close behind him, he hurried up the porch steps to the foreman.

'What do you mean? Why should Grant have been shot? How do you know?'

Howden went back into the cool of the house. Lonnie and Polly looked at one another and quickly followed.

'Grant helped me in a shoot-out with the Fletcher rustling gang. We killed two of the bastards, excuse my language, Miss Polly, but unfortunately Pete Fletcher escaped.'

Lonnie gaped at the man, hardly unable to believe what he was saying. Now he exploded.

'My God! I knew it! Grant can't be trusted five minutes on his own. Especially as he had a gun! Why did you let him help you?'

'It was a sort of accident that he did. He happened to be in the wrong place at the wrong time. But,' Howden shrugged, 'it was Grant's decision to help me.'

'You should have stopped him.'

Howden was thinking the same, although he didn't see how he could have done.

Lonnie paced the floor once or twice, coming back to stand by Polly. 'And now, thanks to you, this Fletcher might have shot him.'

'Not exactly. Because you see that ain't the worst of it.'

'What is it?' Polly could tell the foreman was upset

and she put a hand on his arm.

'Vincent McGrath has been helping the rustlers.'

'Vince! Vince has been betraying his father?' Polly was shocked. She knew Vincent was wild, a bit mad, but she could hardly believe he would do something like that, especially when it was so obvious how much his father loved him.

'I'm afraid so.' Howden nodded. 'And I overheard him and Fletcher cooking up a plan to kill Grant and me . . .'

'You?'

'In revenge for shooting Ricky and George Reece. And I ain't been Vince's favourite person for a long while now. He'd see this as a good excuse to get rid of me, especially as he had Fletcher's help. So I hightailed it out here to warn Grant only to find he ain't around.'

'And you think Vince and Fletcher might have caught up with him and shot him?'

'Well, Miss Polly, they shouldn't have done. He should have got back here long before them but when I first saw Grant he was going hunting. So maybe he decided to do so after he left me and they caught up with him in the mountains. It's the only thing I can think of.'

'This is awful,' Lonnie moaned. He was pale-faced beneath his colourful bruises, looked sick. 'We'll have to go and find him.'

'I was just on my way when I saw you two drawing up outside. Miss Polly, you'd better go back to Salt Creek.'

'Oh.' Polly didn't look too pleased. She wanted to

search for Grant as well.

'Warn Mr Kent and your cousin that there might be trouble. OK?'

Polly didn't argue. She knew what Howden was going to do was man's work. If she insisted on going along the foreman would foolishly feel he'd have to look out for her and wouldn't be able to do his job properly. It might result in him being hurt. And he was right. The people in town needed to know what had happened. Vincent was out of control, could do anything, and so might McGrath once he knew what his son had been up to.

She hugged Lonnie. 'I'm sure Grant is all right.'

'I hope so.'

So did Polly.

Once she'd gone, Howden said: 'You up to coming with me?'

'Yes.' Lonnie was determined. 'But, sir, I haven't got a horse.'

'Never mind. You can ride behind me. It's not far into the mountains.'

'Where's your horse? We didn't see one as we came up.'

'I left it behind the house.' Hid it, in case while he was inside Vincent and Fletcher spotted it and trapped him. 'Come on. It'll be getting dark soon and hard to see.'

And up there, even on the lower slopes of the mountain, it might prove too cold for Grant to survive the night, especially if he was wounded. Howden didn't tell Lonnie that. Lonnie was jittery enough as it was.

It didn't take them long to ride up into the mountains. But it was already deep in shadow under the trees and by the rocks. Howden didn't like it. Anyone could be hiding there, waiting, and he wouldn't see them until it was too late.

'Get down,' he told Lonnie and dismounted as well.

'Grant!' Lonnie called.

'Hush.' Howden snaked out a hand to catch hold of the boy's arm. 'Vince and Fletcher might still be around. We don't want them to hear us.'

'They're not here,' Lonnie began, then stopped with a gasp and said, 'What the hell is that?' And he pointed further up the slope to where in the gloom of some pine trees something moved. Was it a mountain lion? Or a bear? Were they about to be attacked by a wild animal?

But Howden grinned and said, 'It's Grant's horse.'

Lonnie breathed easier. 'Is Grant with it? Can you see him?'

'Let's go, see.'

With Howden clutching his horse's reins, they hurried up the slope. Although a bit restless, Grant's horse remained where it was allowing Howden to catch it up.

'Whoa, boy,' he said, patting its neck.

'Oh God, Mr Howden, look.'

'What is it?'

'There's blood on the saddle.'

Howden saw Lonnie was right. 'Dammit.'

'Has Grant been shot?'

'Well, it sure looks that way.'

'Then where is he?'

Howden looked round. There was no sign of Grant amongst the trees but, of course, his horse could have wandered here from anywhere on the mountain slope. But he probably wasn't far away. The question was where.

Grant thought he must have passed out with the shock and pain. At least when he opened his eyes it seemed much darker than it had been before and he was cold, shivering, thought he had lost a lot of blood. He was still clinging to the tree, his arm feeling numb with the effort. He was scared. What was he going to do? Knew there wasn't much he could do. He shivered some more. Was he going to die out here on the mountain?

And then he heard voices.

Was it Vincent and Fletcher come back to make sure he was dead? No, please . . . he huddled closer into the ground, hoping they wouldn't see him.

And then with a lifting of his heart he recognized Lonnie's voice! And Howden's. He was saved. He would be all right. He opened his mouth to call to them and to his dismay he hardly made a sound, just a sort of croaking noise that would never reach them all that way above him. And he knew they hadn't heard him for their voices were already fading away. If he didn't do something they would move off, not find him.

Then he remembered the gun hanging at his hip. Carefully, not wanting to slide any further down the slope, he reached his hand down to catch hold of the butt. Just as carefully he drew the gun. Raised it. And fired. Once, twice, three times. That was all. The hammer clicked on an empty barrel. If they hadn't heard the three shots he was done for.

'What was that?' Lonnie asked, coming to a stop.

'Shots. It must be Grant. C'mon, it's back this way.'

'Grant, Grant!'

'Careful, watch your step.' Howden could see they were nearing the edge of the mountain. Thought Grant must be below. Didn't want Lonnie following him. 'Grant, where are you?'

There was no more sound. Howden felt his way forward, wishing it was lighter, and came to a halt at the edge. He hunkered down and peered over. Lonnie got down by him.

'Can you see him? Grant, where are you?'

'Yeah, there he is. Hang on, Grant, we'll get you up.' Howden looked at the slope. It didn't seem too steep or too dangerous. He stood up. From the cantle of his saddle he got hold of his lariat, roped one end of it round his waist and tied the other end to the saddle horn.

'What are you doing?' Lonnie asked.

'Going down for him. You stay here. Hold my horse. Make sure it stands as still as possible.'

'Be careful.'

Howden tested the rope to make sure it was secure, then let himself over the edge.

It seemed to take a long time to reach Grant. He bent down by him.

'Can you stand up?'

'I'm not sure,' Grant was shivering uncontrollably now, his teeth chattering.

'Here, let me help you.' Howden got his arms under the boy's arms and pulled him upright, causing Grant to yelp in pain. Howden's own wound suddenly decided to hurt him but he ignored it. 'Now, you'll have to help me, I can't get you to the top by myself. Can you do that?'

Grant nodded.

'Hold on to my belt, that's right, both hands.'

The foreman put an arm round Grant's waist and with the other held out from his body to help him balance he inched his way up the slope, slow step after slow step. As they neared the top, Lonnie leant over to catch hold of Grant and pull him up and over. All three collapsed at the top, out of breath.

OK, Howden thought, one problem solved. But now what the hell were they going to do?

CHAPTER NINETEEN

'Grant, Grant, are you all right?' Lonnie cried, once he'd got his breath back. 'Oh God, you've been shot. Are you hurt, in pain?'

'Hush,' Howden said, pulling the boy away from his brother and helping Grant into a sitting position. 'Let's see.' Gently he began to undo Grant's shirt.

'I thought I was going to die out here,' Grant moaned. 'I didn't see how anyone would come and find me.' He began shivering again and once started didn't seem able to stop.

'It's all right. You're safe now.' Howden sat back on his heels and surveyed the wound high on Grant's chest. 'There now, it don't look too bad.'

'It doesn't?' As far as Grant was concerned the bullet wound hurt like hell. Not only that but he thought he must be covered with bruises from his fall down the mountainside and here was Howden making light of it! It didn't seem fair.

'The bullet is still in there . . .'

Both Grant and Lonnie groaned.

'. . . and will have to be got out. But I don't think

that'll be too difficult. And the wound isn't anywhere likely to be fatal.'

'You're not saying that because I'm going to die, are you?'

'No,' Howden said with a grin. 'You'll be fine.'

'But who's going to get the bullet out?' Lonnie wailed. 'There isn't a doctor in Salt Creek.'

'Don't worry, it won't be the first bullet I've removed. But I can't do it out here in the open. I'll need a fire and some boiling water, a sharp knife and plenty of bandages.'

'Oh God.' Grant closed his eyes. He had a feeling that removing the bullet was going to hurt worse than being shot.

Howden put his arms round Grant, helping him to his feet. 'Grant, who did this?'

'It was Vincent McGrath and that rustler, Fletcher. They both shot at me. They were here waiting for me.'

'I feared as much.'

'They would have finished off the job but they thought I'd fallen to the bottom of the mountain. And I heard Fletcher say he was the one shot Uncle Jethro.'

'I ain't real surprised,' said Howden.

'Mr Howden, what next?' Lonnie asked.

'Best thing is for you to take Grant back to the farm. Get him settled in bed. Start a fire and keep him warm. Can you do that?'

Lonnie nodded.

'Meanwhile I'll ride back to the ranch, get what I need and get a buckboard and come back to you.'

'What do you need a buckboard for?' Grant asked.

'Because after I've gotten the bullet out you should both go into town. Grant, you can rest up there and you'll both be safer too until we get all this sorted out.'

'I want to stay at the farm . . .' Grant began.

Howden interrupted. 'For once in your life, Grant, accept the fact that someone knows better than you do and accept their advice.'

'Yes,' Lonnie said firmly. 'You've behaved stupidly enough as it is.' He paused, then, with a worried frown, added, 'And who is going to believe us that Vincent was not only helping the rustlers but shot someone from ambush?'

Howden lifted Grant on to the back of his horse, ignoring his moan of pain. He looked at Lonnie over his shoulder.

'That's the problem ain't it?'

Morgan McGrath would believe whatever his son said and unfortunately there was no proof of Vincent's guilt. It was something they would have to face when it happened. Right now the important thing was to make sure Grant was doctored.

'Off you go,' Howden said handing the horse's reins to Lonnie. 'And be careful. I'll be as quick as I can.'

It was almost dark when Grant and Lonnie got back to the farm. Lonnie helped Grant down from the horse and then let the animal loose in the corral. Once inside Grant crawled into bed while Lonnie started up the stove. Once it was burning he came to sit by his brother.

'How do you feel?'

'Terrible. Oh, Lon, I'm not sure which was worst. Getting shot, thinking I was going to fall all the way to the bottom of the mountain, or being stuck there unable to move.'

'Mr Howden says you're going to be all right and once you are we can leave here.' Lonnie hoped he could persuade Iris to go back to New York with him. 'Go home.'

'No way.'

Lonnie couldn't believe his ears. 'Oh, Grant, don't be so stubborn. Or stupid. This isn't a dime novel.'

Grant knew that only too well. Dime novel heroes didn't often get shot and if they did they were neither hurt nor scared.

'Next time you might not be so lucky.'

'I'm not giving up what's mine. And the next time I'll be more than ready for Vincent McGrath.'

Howden rode back to the Circle M keeping as much to the trees and rocks as he could, not wanting to be spotted by Vincent and Fletcher. It was rapidly darkening and he didn't think they would be able to see him, probably weren't still looking, but he wasn't about to take any chances.

He wondered if they were still together or whether they had already split up. Doubtless Vincent would want to go back to the ranch in time for dinner, knowing his father would start worrying about where he was if he wasn't there. And presumably Fletcher would consider it wise to hightail it out of the area. On the other hand Fletcher had nothing to lose in staying around for a while longer in order to try and kill him, Howden, and Vincent was mad enough when he lost his temper to do anything. Especially with Fletcher urging him on.

Howden was unable to imagine what was going to happen next. But he knew things couldn't go on as they were. He wished he'd done what he'd wanted to do and left the ranch already. He wanted to remain loyal to Morgan McGrath but he didn't see how that would now be possible.

He was almost at the ranch when he came to a halt. Something was going on. Lamps were burning out by the barn and by their light he could see several of the cowboys gathered there; some were talking, others saddling up horses. And McGrath was there as well, his bulky figure unmistakable. What were they doing? Howden had a bad feeling about it.

Slowly so no one heard him, he urged his horse forward, bending to stroke its neck so it didn't make any noise. He had almost reached the barn when McGrath stepped in front of his men.

'Let's go get 'em,' he yelled. 'No one shoots at my son and gets away with it.'

Howden's heart skipped a beat. This was really bad. The rancher had to be talking about Grant and Lonnie. Vincent must have come back to the ranch and spun a story, rousing his father to quick anger. McGrath was a fair man but wanting the Cunninghams' land and their water, he would be even more ready than usual to believe whatever Vincent told him. And now he was leading some of his wilder hands to go after the boys, who wouldn't stand a chance against them. It would be as good as murder.

Howden decided he had neither time nor chance to convince McGrath he was wrong. Quite likely Vincent had poisoned his father against his foreman at the same time. He glanced quickly at the men. Vincent wasn't amongst them. So where was he?

Unable to sit still, listening to his brother's lunacy any longer, Lonnie stood up and went over to the window. Suddenly he stiffened.

'What's the matter?' Grant asked.

Lonnie turned back to him, his face white.

'It looks like you're going to get your wish sooner than you thought.'

'Why?'

'There're two riders out there. And one of them is Vincent McGrath.'

CHAPTER TWENTY

'Oh hell!' Grant found his heart missing several beats. 'Are you sure?'

'Yeah.'

'Do they know we're here?'

'They must do. The horse is in the corral and . . .'

And there was the light in the bedroom. Quickly Grant leant over and blew it out, plunging the room into darkness. He wasn't sure if he was frightened or excited. Probably a little bit of both.

'Help me up,' he said.

He tried not to moan as Lonnie put his arms round him and helped him out of the bed. Luckily the room was so small that the window was only a couple of steps away. Keeping to one side of the window, hoping he wouldn't be spotted, Grant peered out. There was no mistake.

Vincent McGrath and Pete Fletcher.

'Perhaps they'll go away,' Lonnie said hopefully.

No chance of that. The next moment both of the men started shooting at the farmhouse. Bullets smacked into the walls.

'Dammit!' Grant jumped back and slammed the

ill-fitting shutter across the window; just in time, as a bullet hit it, making the wood shudder. 'Did you bolt the door when we came in?'

'I shut it but I don't know if I bolted it.' Lonnie's voice was trembling.

'Go and make sure. Secure the other shutters. Go on. Hurry.'

As Lonnie ran out of the room, Grant opened the shutter a little way, risking a glance out. Vincent and Fletcher were still sitting on their horses a little way off from the house. It was obvious they didn't quite know what to do, didn't know for sure who was in the house, perhaps thought they only had Lonnie to deal with. That might just give him and his brother an edge, not much of a one, but the only one they were likely to get. He wished Howden hadn't gone back to the ranch but had come here with them.

The holster with its gun lay at the end of the bed. One hand holding his wound, Grant reached for it.

'Everything's bolted down,' Lonnie said, coming back into the room. 'Grant, what are we going to do?' He stared at the gun in his brother's hand. 'Are you planning on using that?'

'What choice have I got? I will if I have to. You and me didn't start this fight, we've done nothing wrong but that doesn't mean anything to Vincent or Fletcher and neither of them will hesitate to shoot us if they can, you understand that, don't you Lon?'

Lonnie nodded.

'I know you don't like it but it's the way it is.'

Lonnie nodded again. 'Don't worry, Grant, I'll manage. I wonder where Mr Howden is?'

'Just what I was wondering. But I doubt if he could have got to the ranch and be anywhere close yet, especially driving a buckboard. It's just us two on our own.'

'I know.'

'Is the shotgun loaded?'

'I'll go and see.'

'Fetch it in here.'

Grant glanced out of the window again. The men had gone but not far because their horses were still there.

'Be careful, Lonnie,' he called a warning. 'They're up to something.'

'Hey, you, in there!' That was Vincent McGrath.

It seemed the rancher's son was over by the half-finished hut, although Grant couldn't be sure.

'Come on out and if you promise to give up your claim to the farm I promise I'll let you go.'

'Don't believe the bastard,' Grant said to Lonnie. His brother was standing in the bedroom doorway clutching the shotgun in his hands, with an undecided look in his eyes as if he might take Vincent up on his offer.

'You know your brother's dead, don't you?'

So they did think Lonnie was alone. Good.

'There's nothing for you here. You can't handle the farm on your own.'

Vincent was by the hut. Grant could see him now. Fletcher wasn't there with him. Where was he?

'Come on, you stupid sonofabitch I'm giving you an offer you can't refuse.' Vincent's voice rose as he lost his temper. 'You can't win against me. Take it or leave it. I'm counting to twenty. If you don't come out by then by God I'm coming in after you.'

Vincent was up to some trick. Grant didn't believe for one minute in the offer he was making. He would hardly confess to killing one Cunningham brother to the other and then let him go. Yet for some reason he was wasting time, trying to keep Lonnie's attention on him. Why?

Suddenly a shadow dashed up the porch steps. Before Grant could even cry out a warning, Fletcher kicked the flimsy door open. It flew inwards with a crash and a flurry of dust.

'Watch out!' Grant yelled.

Fletcher began firing. Bullets flew everywhere, whining off walls, thumping into the floor.

Grant brought the gun up. But from where he stood he could only see Fletcher's shadow and he didn't have a target.

Fletcher half-turned and saw Lonnie in the bedroom doorway. He grinned. And aimed his gun, finger pulling the trigger.

Lonnie acted instinctively. He dived to the floor. The bullet whined over his head and slammed into the leg of the bed.

Frantically Grant stepped forward, knowing the next bullet wouldn't miss his brother.

But Fletcher didn't have the chance to fire it.

Lonnie raised the shotgun and pulled both triggers.

The boom was much much louder indoors than outside. The buckshot hit Fletcher square on. It picked him up, carried him half-way across the room and flung him down in the corner, a bundle of rags and blood.

'Pete! Pete!' Grant heard Vincent calling out above the echoing noise of the shotgun. 'What's going on?'

Beyond any doubt Fletcher was dead, was going to pose no more danger. Grant went back to the window. Vincent had stood up. Moved out into the open.

'Fletcher's dead!' Grant yelled. 'You're finished.'

'Grant?'

'That's right, I'm still alive.'

'Not for long, goddamn you!'

Grant was never sure what made Vincent do what he did next. Perhaps he truly was mad, or perhaps he was mad because he couldn't stand the thought of another failure. Maybe he feared he would have to face the law for what he had done. Whatever the reason he suddenly started walking forward, shooting as he came.

'Vince, stop there!'

Vincent took no notice. He was almost at the house when his gun ran out of bullets. He threw it away and reached for his second. His face was twisted with fury and his eyes did indeed hold a look of madness. Grant shivered. Vincent was not going to come to his senses and give up.

'Grant,' Lonnie said uncertainly from behind him.

Footsteps loud in the sudden quiet, Vincent climbed deliberately up the porch steps.

Grant moved away from the bed and, gritting his teeth against the bullet wound, stepped by Lonnie into the living-room, just as Vincent entered the house.

They both raised their guns at the same time. Vincent fired, twice, quickly. Grant remembered Polly's words of advice and took careful aim. Shot once. Both of Vincent's bullets went wide. Grant's didn't. It struck Vincent full in the chest and he staggered backwards out on to the porch and down the steps, stumbling to the ground. His legs twitched and then he was still. He wouldn't move again.

Shaking, Grant put the gun down on the table. He was aware of Lonnie coming up behind him.

'Oh, God, Grant, now the hell what? We've killed Vincent McGrath!'

CHAPTER TWENTY-ONE

Before Grant could answer, they both heard the sound of a horse being ridden hard. Apprehensively they glanced up.

'Grant! Lonnie!'

'It's Mr Howden,' Lonnie said in relief. Then relief turned to apprehension. 'I thought he was coming back in a buckboard.'

The man drew his horse to a halt, so that it almost went down on its haunches, and was flinging himself off before it had come to a stop.

'Grant!' he shouted breathlessly. 'McGrath is coming with a bunch of . . . oh Jesus! Is that Vince? Oh my God.'

'Yes, I shot him. Fletcher is inside,' Grant said. 'He's dead too. The two of them came here thinking to surprise Lonnie on his own. Mr Howden, we had no choice.'

Howden nodded, as if he realized that. 'There's no time . . .' he began.

But then there was no time for anything. McGrath

and his men appeared round the bend in the hill. They would be at the house any moment.

'Mr Howden,' Lonnie said, very frightened.

'Don't worry. Get in the house. Let me handle this.'

'No,' Grant said. 'This is our trouble more than yours.'

Howden wanted to tell him not to argue, that he was wounded and in no state to stand up for himself, but there wasn't time for that either. McGrath, flanked by the seven or eight cowboys with him, came to a stop in front of the house. Quickly Howden stepped in front of the Cunninghams.

'Brad! What the hell are you doing here?' McGrath said.

Then he saw the body of his son lying on the ground. For a moment there was a silence so deep that it was possible to hear the sound of the creek running through its banks. With a little cry the rancher dismounted.

'Vince! Vince!' He ran over to his son, bending down by him. 'Oh no! No!'

Howden put out a hand towards the cowboys, hoping they wouldn't make any rash moves. He only hoped Grant wouldn't do anything stupid either.

McGrath stood up, his eyes glistening with tears and fury.

'You bastards! You've killed my son!' His hand went towards his gun.

'Wait a minute, Mr McGrath,' Howden said. 'This ain't how it seems.'

'What do you mean? These bastards have shot

Vincent. They had it in for him from the beginning and now they've killed him. Why are you sticking up for them?'

'They had no choice. Vince had already shot Grant from ambush and then he and Fletcher came here to finish the job by shooting Lonnie.'

'I don't believe you.'

'It's true,' Grant said. 'I can show you my wound if you like.'

'Grant! Shut up and let me handle this. I'm sorry, Mr McGrath, it's true.'

'And what the hell are you talking about saying Vince came here with Fletcher? You mean one of the rustlers? What would Vince be doing with him?'

Howden said sadly, 'I'm real sorry, Mr McGrath, but Vince was supplying Pete Fletcher with information about your cattle in return for money.'

McGrath gave a short angry bark of laughter. 'Don't be ridiculous.'

'Then why is Fletcher's body inside?' Grant said.

'Because you two bastards were in with the rustlers and Vince came here to stop you.'

'How could that be?' Howden asked. 'The rustling has been going on much longer than these boys have been here.'

'They must have taken after their uncle.' McGrath suddenly let out a yell. 'This is damn nonsense! These sonsofbitches have killed my boy and for some reason, Howden, you, someone I trusted and thought of as another son, are taking their side. Well, I came here to string up those two and I can string you up as well.'

'Mr McGrath, listen to sense. Why would I lie? Look at the evidence.'

McGrath swore nastily.

Grant looked at Lonnie. McGrath wasn't about to listen. They were going to die.

Then one of the younger cowboys, one of those Lonnie recognized as having helped beat him up, said, 'What Mr Howden says is true.' He blushed bright red as everyone turned to look at him.

'Tell him,' Howden urged.

'Vince boasted of helping the Fletcher gang. Said it was the only way to get easy money to spend. And he said he wanted to kill the two Cunningham boys, was plotting to make you believe they were rustlers so you would lynch them. I'm real sorry, sir, but that's the truth.'

For a moment, even then, McGrath might still have drawn his gun, taken matters into his own hands. But he didn't. With a shudder that seemed to rack his whole body, he hung his head.

'Brad, bring my boy home so I can bury him.'

A few days later Howden rode up to where Grant was taking it easy on the porch. He dismounted and walked up the steps to stand in the shade.

'How are you?'

'Bullet out, patched up and getting better,' Grant said with a smile.

From the house came the sound of a girl humming a tune. Howden smiled in return as he recognized the voice as belonging to Polly Summers.

'Polly is looking after me real fine.'

'I bet. She's a nice girl. Deserves a better life than working in her cousin's saloon.'

'I know.'

'Where's Lonnie?'

'He's gone into Salt Creek to get some supplies and talk to Iris. He's going to tell her that he'll have to stay out here with me for a while until I'm better and we get properly settled, then he wants to go into town and help her father run the store. He's not a farmer and will never make one.'

'All come out right then?'

'Yes, I guess. I'm sorry for what happened though.'

Howden nodded. 'It wasn't your fault.'

'I know but both Lonnie and me killed a man and although it was self-defence, somehow that doesn't make it easier to accept.'

'There's no easy way to live with it but live with it you'll have to.'

Grant knew that but he thought it was going to be a long time before he stopped having nightmares.

'Mr Howden?'

'Yeah?'

'What about Mr McGrath?'

'You won't be bothered by him any more.'

'That isn't what I meant. I meant, is he all right? How is he coping with his loss? What do you mean, he won't bother us?'

'Mr McGrath has left.'

'Left?' Grant sat up straight in surprise. 'Left the Circle M?'

'Yeah. He felt nothing remained there for him. Couldn't face life there day after day without Vince.

He's gone back south to Atlanta where he has family.'

'I'm sorry.'

'Me too. He was a good man. He deserved better.'

'What's going to happen to his ranch?'

'He left it to me.'

'Oh! Oh, I'm pleased for you.'

'I just wish it had been under different circumstances but, hell, Grant, I know I'll make a better boss than Vincent ever could have done. And most of the hands have said they'll stop on and help. And, Grant, don't worry, no way will I try and take over your farm.' Howden smiled, almost shyly. 'I'm hoping we can be good neighbours.'

'I'm sure we can.' Grant sat back and surveyed the land. 'There's room for us all out here. Come on in and tell Polly the news.'